ALSO BY
RONALD J. LEWIS

FICTION

Murder in Mackinac
(Agawa Press)

Terror at the Soo Locks
(Agawa Press)

BUSINESS

Activity-Based Models for Cost Management Systems
(QUORUM BOOKS—SIMON & SCHUSTER)

Activity-Based Costing for Marketing and Manufacturing
(QUORUM BOOKS—GREENWOOD PUBLISHING)

Cost Accounting
(GINN PRESS)

Cost Accounting (Co-author with K. Most)
(WILEY PUBLISHING)

Mackinaw Honolulu CONNECTION

A NOVEL

Ronald J. Lewis

Agawa Press
Mackinaw City, Michigan

Additional copies of this book may be ordered through book-stores or by sending $12.95 plus $3.50 for postage and handling to:

Agawa Press
Box 39
Mackinaw City, MI 49701
(616) 436-7032

Copyright © 1998 by Ronald J. Lewis
Cover and map illustrations by Mary Blue
Cover design by Eric Norton
Text design by Mary Jo Zazueta
Library of Congress Catalog Card Number: 98-72209
ISBN: 0-9642436-2-8

Printed in the United States of America
10 9 8 7 6 5 4 3 2 1

To my wife, Margie,
whose Finnish heritage became a part of me.
To my three sons, Jeff, Randy, and Gary,
who are a blessing to me.
And to all the American war veterans, who
preserved this wonderful free country for us.

ACKNOWLEDGMENTS

I would like to thank the following persons for supplying information for *Mackinaw-Honolulu Connection*. It was important to me to make sure that every action necessary to the plot was technically possible, and logistically plausible. These are the people, or groups, who verified the accuracy of selected parts of my fictional narrative.

U.S. Coast Guard, Sault Ste. Marie

U.S. Coast Guard, Cheboygan

U.S. Coast Guard, St. Ignace

Chief Dennis Bradley, Mackinaw Island Fire Department

Albert G. Ballert, Great Lakes Commission, Ann Arbor

Russ Veihl, Deputy Sherriff, Cheboygan County

Lee H. Belles and Larry M. Belles, who served on the *Edgar B. Speer*, the *Roger Blough*, and other Great Lakes freighters.

MACKINAW — HONOLULU
Connection

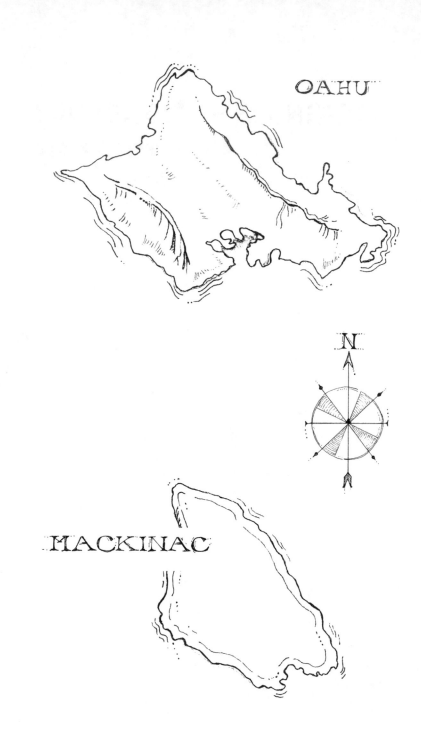

OAHU

N

MACKINAC

1.

Tuesday, June 2

It was foggy on the Straits of Mackinac. The *Malaga Badra*, a six-hundred foot foreign freighter registered in Bangkok, was proceeding slowly eastward at twelve knots under the Mackinac Bridge at three-thirty in the morning. The fog was unyielding, making it difficult for the lake pilot, required to steer foreign ships in the Great Lakes, to see more than a few hundred feet. Under these conditions it would be impossible to stop a ship if something unexpectedly appeared in its path.

On deck, out of sight of anyone in the pilothouse four decks above, a slender figure dashed from the lower cabin section on deck toward the starboard side of the ship. A stocky crewman leaped out of a shadowy passageway in pursuit. The crewman lunged out desperately and caught an ankle, sending the figure crashing to the deck. The sailor cap flew off, revealing a woman's long blonde hair. As she looked up into his menacing Peter Lorre face, the crewman raised his arm revealing a knife in his right hand. Before the knife could come down the woman jabbed her knuckles into his eyes, and scraped her fingernails blood deep into the side of his cheeks.

It gave her enough time to get up and race to the rail. The crewman struggled to his feet, and caught up with her just as she placed both hands on the rail. Without compunction, he plunged the knife deep into her back. She winced painfully, but managed to climb up on the railing and dive into the churning waters.

The ominous crewman mumbled a few inaudible words, turned around and disappeared into the darkness of the ship's hold. He did not notice the figure of a man who had been peering out from behind a lifeboat.

At this moment the *Malaga Badra* had reached the narrowest section of the Straits between Mackinac Island and Round Island. The woman survived the fall into the cool water, and struggled frantically to swim the short distance to the rocky beach surrounding Round Island Lighthouse.

Her body shivered as she reached out for a large protruding rock. She pulled herself out of the water, and crawled along the craggy beach. In a last desperate lunge she collapsed on a layer of small stones. A thin stream of blood trickled down her back, as the last remnants of life slowly dwindled away.

O

A FEW HOURS LATER, AT SEVEN-THIRTY THAT MORNING, SEVERAL ferry boats departed on schedule from the Mackinaw City and St. Ignace docks, headed for Mackinac Island. The first to round the curve into the narrow channel between Mackinac Island and Round Island that morning was a Star Lines ferry, from Mackinaw City, with its distinctive rooster tail sailing high in the air. Captain John Trudeau, a veteran pilot on the Straits, was at the helm, squinting for a better view as he heard the foghorns blaring threateningly at him.

The only bad dreams Captain Trudeau ever had were those of the one thousand-foot ore carrier, the *Stewart J. Cort*, coming down the center of this narrow passageway, in a dense fog. In his nightmare, his comparatively tiny ferry-boat would plod directly into its path, plunge helplessly under the mighty bow, and disappear into the deep.

But, when he was awake at the helm, he was always assured by the fact that after thousands of crossings it had never happened to any ferry boat on the Straits. An assurance that was due to the meticulous care of the Great Lakes pilots, the Coast Guard, and the ferry boat captains.

O

THIS MORNING AS CAPTAIN TRUDEAU PILOTED THE *STARLIGHT* cautiously between the two islands, he spotted a human figure on the stony beach surrounding the base of the Round Island Lighthouse. He notified the Commander of the Coast Guard station in St. Ignace, Perry Grant.

"Perry, looks like there's a body at the Round Island Lighthouse. It's not moving. Ya'd better check it out.... just in case it's still alive. I can't really tell if it's a man or woman. I can see what looks like long blonde hair.... but you know those young punks with their long hair all look like girls.... so ya can't tell which."

The Coast Guard sent the *Biscayne Bay*, a one-hundred-forty foot cutter and ice breaker to the site within minutes.

Commander Perry Grant was in his late fifties. His clean-shaven face was grizzled and tanned from frequent exposure to wind and sun. He was getting a little paunchy, but still looked neat in his uniform. He boarded a small motorized raft with younger Guardsman, Dan Mason. They landed as close as they could to the Lighthouse and walked over to the body. The battered body was face down in a flat area of small stones that bordered the Lighthouse.

"My God, look at that knife," Perry said, rolling the lifeless body over carefully, so as not to dislodge the knife. "Looks like a young woman, all right.... we better not touch anything until the police get here."

"Who the heck has jurisdiction over Round Island, Commander?" Dan asked. There had never been problems of this nature in the Mackinac area as long as Dan could remember.

O

REINO ASUMA, SHERIFF OF MACKINAC COUNTY, WAS TRYING TO create some Finnish pancakes his mother had often fixed when he was still living at home. His imitative efforts were a mere reflection of the scrumptious popover-like results his mother would elicit.... but nevertheless worth every second of his time, when he covered them with butter and genuine maple syrup.

Sheriff Reino Asuma was a powerful brute of a man,

which perhaps had some bearing on his becoming a law-enforcement officer. He had wavy, although thinning, blonde hair, and was generally considered good looking, but not handsome, by the girls who admired him. The going joke at the Mackinac County Building in St. Ignace was that a big brown bear came into town one day, took one look at Reino, and scampered back into the woods. The fact that no bears have wandered into St. Ignace since Reino took office made the tale somewhat believable.

His parents, both born in the Upper Peninsula of Michigan, were pure Finns. After two years taking general requirements at Lake Superior State University in Sault Ste. Marie, Michigan, he became interested in law enforcement, finished his bachelor's degree, and joined the local police department. He became the Chief of Police in Sault Ste. Marie in 1993.

In 1996, he resigned and became the Sheriff of Mackinac County. The Sheriff's Office is located in the County Building in St. Ignace. Reino loved the Mackinac Straits area, and bought a cottage along the Straits just two miles west of the magnificent Mackinac Bridge.

The call came from Commander Perry Grant. "Reino, we got what looks like a murder here on Round Island.... a woman with a knife in her back. That sounds like murder ..... don't ya think! It's your jurisdiction, isn't it?"

"Yep, it sure is. I'll be right there....as soon as I can.... that is."

"Listen Reino, if you go straight to the Coast Guard Station.... I'll send a launch for you," Perry offered.

"Thanks Perry. I'll be leaving in about ten minutes."

Reino wanted to finish his Finnish pancakes, so he gobbled them down as fast as he could and headed for the
docks. Before he left he called Oscar Bobay, the Mackinac
County medical examiner. Oscar, who had been an M.D.
from Wayne State University, was an excellent pathologist.

He had spent most of his life in Northern Michigan. His
family had French roots that dated back before the Revo-
lution. His original name was probably Beaubait, but was
shortened by some ancestor along the historical route to
Bobay.

Oscar had recently moved to St. Ignace from Sault Ste.
Marie, where he had been the medical examiner. Reino,
who as Chief of Police, had depended on him so much at
the Sault, had recommended him for the position.

"Meet me at the Coast Guard Station docks right away,
Oscar. We got ourselves a real murder.... according to
Perry."

"Okay, okay, Reino. I'll meet ya there as fast as I can."

O

THE LAUNCH DELIVERED THE TWO MEN AT THE ROUND ISLAND
Lighthouse forty-five minutes later. They proceeded to
examine the body and ask questions. Oscar formally pronounced that the woman was dead. To Reino's dismay, no
one had witnessed, or could offer any explanation for, the
apparent murder.

"Oscar.... I'm going to call Sam. He might at least have
some ideas. You remember how he and Brad Kendall were
so helpful in that bombing of that foreign ship at the Soo
Locks back in ninety-six?"

Sam Green was the FBI agent stationed in Detroit and assigned to Northern Michigan. He was Afro-American, brought up on Detroit's West Side. He had been a star football player for Mackenzie High in 1971-72, still maintaining his trim, muscular shape over the years. He never married, probably because he realized that he would make a poor husband. His job was extremely dangerous, often involving undercover assignments. His hours were completely indeterminate, because he didn't like to assign the tough jobs to the less experienced agents. And he just couldn't resist being in on the exciting cases.

That evening on the six o'clock news the story broke. Dave and Pallas on Traverse City's Channel 7 & 4 announced that a woman's body was discovered at the Round Island Lighthouse, across from Mackinac Island, at approximately seven-thirty in the morning by the captains of both the Star and Arnold ferry boat lines. Reino wouldn't give them too many details, yet.

2.

◆ SAM GREEN WAS AT HIS OFFICE IN DOWNTOWN
Detroit when he received the call the next morning.

"Allo Sam, this is Reino.... ya know.... da sheriff from da UP."

Reino loved to over exaggerate his Upper Peninsula, Yoopanite.... he called it.... accent. When he was younger he was embarrassed by downstate friends who kidded him about the Finglish idiosyncrasies in his speech. Since he had now eliminated most of them from his vocabulary, he subconsciously wanted to remind others of his Finnish heritage. After all, Finland was the only nation ever to pay back its world war debt to the United States, and had the highest literacy rate in the world for most of the twentieth century.

"Of course I know! Who else would be named Reino?

I'll bet I already know exactly what you are calling about, Reino. The woman at the Straits.... right?"

"Right. I need your help. There's nothin'! No purse.... nothin" to ID her.... just a knife, and what's left of her clothes. And Oscar said she had water in her lungs. So she could've come from a passing ship. That puts her in your jurisdiction..... doesn't it..... eh? Can you get your lab to help? I'd appreciate it, Sam."

"Okay Reino. I'm going to classify this as a possible interstate crime. I'll fly up to the Pellston Airport tomorrow with a team. Meet us at ten with some transportation. There's nothing hot here in Detroit right now.... and you know I love Mackinaw City. Any excuse to go there.... whoops..... don't quote me on that! This really does sound like more than a local murder. There's virtually no major crime in your region, so I think there's more to it.... maybe even international implications."

"Thanks Sam. I'll be there at ten. And I'll call Brad Kendall. If it's anything international he can get in touch with George for us over in Honolulu."

"Great.... I'd love to see Brad again. I haven't seen him since the bombing of the *Singapore Soo* at the locks."

○

REINO CALLED BRAD AT HIS PARENT'S COTTAGE IN MACKINAW City, after getting the usual *leave a message at the beep-beep* at Brad's house in Sault Ste. Marie. Bradley Kendall was a professor of Accounting at Lake Superior State University (LSSU) at the Sault. He and Reino had become good friends. His family had lived in a waterfront cottage in

Mackinaw City, on the Straits of Mackinac just west of, and in full view of, the Mackinac Bridge when he was born.

Later the family lived in Ann Arbor when Bradley's father became a professor of Engineering at the University of Michigan. They kept the cottage as a summer home. His mother and father preferred to live in Florida after retirement, so Brad spent the summers at the cottage whenever possible.

After finishing high school, Brad attended Northern Michigan University in Marquette. He received his bachelor's degree in Accounting in 1982. Two years later he finished an MBA at Central Michigan University. Then in 1992, he finished his Ph.D. at the University of Michigan. He professed at Michigan State University for a while, and then joined the faculty at LSSU at the Sault in 1996.

"Allo Brad."

"Allo Reino," Brad quickly responded with his Finglish imitation of Reino. "What's up?"

"Did you hear the report of the murder on the news last night?"

"No. I was trying to write a journal article. Publish or perish.... you know."

"Well, a woman's body was found next to the Round Island Lighthouse early yesterday morning. John Trudeau saw it first.... you know.... he's a captain on the Star Lines."

"Sure, I know John."

"An Arnold Lines *Cat* was a few seconds behind, and their crew spotted the body, too. Anyway, I'll tell you all about it tomorrow. Can you go with me to pick up Sam

Green at the Pellston Airport? He's coming with a team to help identify the woman."

"Okay. I'd like to see Sam again. But, won't I be out of place with an official investigation going on?"

"Nope! Sam said to include you. In case it has any international implications. It could.... if a foreign ship were involved. Remember that Russian ship a few years back in Lake Michigan? One of the crew members was found dead.... body washed up on shore near Petoskey.... or somewhere in the area. And.... I think Sam just wants to see us both again."

3.

◆ REINO AND BRAD DROVE THE FIFTEEN MILES FROM Mackinaw to the Pellston Airport arriving just in time to see the twin engine Lear jet glide onto the runway. Sam deplaned alone.

"Hey Sam, where's your team?"

"Hello Reino." Sam thrust out his powerful right hand to each man. "Great to see you too Brad. The lab team decided to drive their equipment truck.... just in case they need something special. They'll stay overnight at the Hamilton Inn, and begin working tomorrow morning."

"I'll arrange everything for them tomorrow, Sam." Reino said. "I knew they couldn't do much today, anyway. Oscar Bobay examined the body and is expecting them at the county morgue in St. Ignace. You know Oscar.... he'll be a great help to them."

As they approached the main corner of Central and

Nicolet, with its new big-city display of fancy traffic lights, Reino said. "Let's get lunch. I'll treat!"

Reino was always hungry, thought Brad.

"Good idea," Sam said. "How about Darrow's or Audie's? They're my two favorites."

"I just ate at Darrow's," Reino informed them. "So let's go to Audie's. Okay Brad?"

"I'm neutral. I like 'em both," Brad tacitly assented, as if he had something else on his mind.

Reino gobbled up a whitefish sandwich as if he never had one before. After lunch the three men drove to Brad's cottage.

"What a view!" Sam exclaimed as he looked out the panoramically arranged Pella windows enclosing the front porch facing the Straits of Mackinac. The water was a deep blue, with small whitecaps breaking on the shore. In the breathtaking view was the magnificent Mackinac Bridge, with the Grand Hotel on Mackinac Island in the background. The bridge was about two miles away, and Mackinac Island was about eight miles in the distance. From Brad's porch the Grand Hotel could be seen just to the right of the south anchor pier.

Reino, trying to imitate Brad when he bragged about the bridge, said, "You know, Sam, that although some people use the span between the towers, the length of a suspension bridge should be measured by the distance between the two anchor piers. The suspension portion, between Piers 17 and 22, of the five-mile long Mighty Mac is 8,614 feet, making it the longest suspension bridge in the world."

Brad had to add, even though he was sad to do so,

"You're right Reino, though I'm sorry to say that there are two suspension bridges being built right now, one in Japan and one in Denmark, that are expected to be longer than the Mackinac Bridge. But.... look at the Empire State Building.... then the Sears Tower. They used to be the world's tallest buildings. Now I heard that there is not just one, but two buildings in Kuala Lumpur, Malaysia, that are taller than the Sears Tower."

The three men sat down on the porch. Brad seemed anxious to start a new conversation.

"I talked to George in Honolulu last night. He was very interested in the fact that a woman's body was found in the Straits of Mackinac, close to a shipping channel. He thinks he might be able to help us identify her."

George Tong, owner of the famed Kahana Hotel and Restaurant in Honolulu, was the brains behind the Information Network System (INS). He used the abandoned Wo Fat's restaurant building, famous from the "Hawaii Five-O" program, in downtown Honolulu, as his operations headquarters.

He had developed a communications system that was capable of tracing criminal activities anywhere in the world. Because it is on an isolated island, Honolulu is unique from all other American cities. The INS was used to monitor the movement of international criminals into Hawaii, particularly into Honolulu. The main concern, originally, was drug traffic, but the system was capable of exposing all forms of illicit activity.

Information is funneled to George who distributes it, wherever necessary. INS never does anything illegal, and merely transmits the information to the police when the situation calls for action. The group had an unofficial approval from the State of Hawaii.

It became so successful in Hawaii, and in several other cooperating U.S. states, that the Secretary General of the United Nations gave it unofficial approval to operate internationally, as long as it had agreement from the national governments involved.

It was then that George found out about the Couriers. There were only twenty Couriers in the world. They originated as a result of the nuclear threat at the end of World War II. The United States, Great Britain, the USSR, China, France, and the other major nations developed a top secret communications system. They were deathly afraid that there would be an accidental nuclear missile attack.... the result of faulty or slow communications.

It was Winston Churchill's idea to have each leader, of the twenty nations that agreed to the plan, to select a Courier. No one else in the hierarchy was to know who their Courier was. President Truman and Prime Minister Churchill selected their nations' first Couriers. President Kennedy depended heavily on his Courier during the Cuban crisis.

The Couriers transmitted personally written messages from one leader to another. They had identification codes that were known only to the twenty leaders. They traveled and behaved like normal travelers or tourists to remain anonymous. If they had to expose their identity as a Courier, because of an immediate nuclear or other crisis, a replacement Courier had to be selected.

With the end of the Cold War between the Communist Bloc and the Free Enterprise Nations, the Couriers were assigned to other crises, like the Gulf War and Iraq's continuing threat to peace in the Middle East. With the agreement of the Secretary General of the United Nations, all of the member nations with Couriers made them available to George and the INS.

The American Courier was assigned by the President to assist George's INS operation on an as needed basis. George never made personal contact with the Courier.... he was given a telephone number at the White House to leave a message for the Courier.

Both Sam and Brad were original members of the INS team, and Reino was involved after the bombing of the freighter, *Singapore Soo*, at the Soo Locks in 1996.

"George said that a young woman on his INS team, named Ingra Jensen, has not responded to his request for information. She was on a foreign freighter, and was supposed to report in yesterday.... but she didn't. He asked me to trace a ship registered in Bangkok named the *Malaga Badra*. George hasn't heard from her since she left Honolulu, where she boarded."

"Why don't you call Al Ballert down in Ann Arbor? He can trace it for you. He traces the foreign ships for the Great Lakes Commission," Sam suggested.

"Or Commander Gilbert, the operations officer at the Soo," Reino added. "Either one would know just about where the *Malabra*.... or whatever you called it.... is."

"I keep in touch with Al Ballert. I'll give him a call right now," Brad decided.

After a short conversation with Al, Brad reported. "Al said that the *Malaga Badra* should have passed through the Straits sometime after midnight on Tuesday.... let's see.... that would be June second."

Reino practically shouted, "That's it.... that's it. John Trudeau, and the Arnold Line crew spotted the body that same morning."

"That means it could be George's team member.... this Ingra Jensen could be the one.... but why?" Sam rhetorically asked, not expecting any better answer than he could offer himself.

Brad added, "George didn't say what kind of a mission she was on.... but if she doesn't report in soon, we can assume that the woman's body is that of this Ingra Jensen. I have to teach at Hickam Air Force Base in Hawaii again for three weekends. In fact.... I'll be flying out of Lansing next Thursday. So I'll meet with George right away and see if we can help. I know that if Ingra doesn't report in, he'll want all three of us to work on the team to find out why. You know George. If this gal worked for him, and was murdered.... she didn't just accidentally fall off that ship.... I'm sure.... then there's something big going on."

"Oh you poor fellow," Reino chided. "Did I hear you say you *have to* teach in Hawaii.... what a sacrifice!"

Brad had a habit of saying he *had* to teach in Hawaii, which he had done for Central Michigan University several times.

He wrote his own textbook on *Management Accounting*, which was used in a required course in the Master of Science in Administration (MSA) program. So the

University was happy to have the author of the text, himself, teach the course. It was offered at many U.S. military bases. Brad first taught at the Jacksonville Naval Air Station, and at the Charleston Air Force Base. Now he preferred to teach in the Hawaiian bases, for obvious reasons.

When he would casually say, "I have to teach in Hawaii," most people would respond, "*you have to* teach in Hawaii?"

"Well, we all know what's next." Sam got back to business. "We can't tell anyone anything pertaining to George's INS operation. The news would turn it into a circus. If my lab team doesn't find anything definite to identify the body as someone else, I'm going to stall the investigation until we are sure it is George's secret agent.... whoops.... I don't like the ominous sound of secret agent. I mean George's *team member*. Then, if it is, I'll announce that the unidentified body is that of a tourist. I can't say that she drowned.... with a knife seen sticking out of her back. And, if possible, we must keep the foreign connection out of it. I'll just play dumb and keep stalling.... until the news gets cold."

"You could suggest that it might be a spurned lover, who threw her off a private sailboat or cabin cruiser," Reino said.

"That's a good one, Reino. I'll use it, especially if that local news girl, what's her name .... you know.... wasn't she your whatcha-ma-callit?"

"She was just an old friend, Sam. Not a whatcha-ma-callit."

The whatcha-ma-callit was TV Channel 7 & 4's local news reporter, Susan Young. Susan and Reino had grown up together in the Soo. They were in the same grade and went through grade school and high school together. They were more like brother and sister, according to Reino.

The three friends ended their meeting. Sam Green resumed the official FBI investigation with the cooperation of Sheriff Reino Asuma, representing the local jurisdiction. Both had the cooperation of the Coast Guard Commander, Perry Grant, and the Mackinaw City Police Chief, Wilbert Erbe.

4.

THE *MALAGA BADRA* HAD SAILED PAST THE MACKINAC
Bridge early Tuesday morning, and was scheduled
to reach the Soo Locks by eleven a.m. The
American pilot was Rick Slaker, who lived in Sault Ste.
Marie. Captain Tan Wo Lin was standing beside him at the
helm. The fog began to lift as the ship approached the
mouth of the St. Mary's River at Detour.

"Well, Captain Tan." Rick knew from experience with
many Asian ship captains that Tan was his last name, even
though written first according to Chinese custom. He never
did figure out if his first name was just Wo, or Wo Lin, however. "I would normally leave you at Detour, but since I
would have to hitch a ride up to the Sault anyway, the
Pilots Association allows me to take you all the way."

Pilots would normally be changed at Detour, where a
river pilot would replace the lake pilot. Sixteen miles on the
other side of the Soo Locks a lake pilot would take over
again. Exceptions were made for Pilot Slaker, when ships,

like the *Malaga Badra,* were destined for Algoma Steel, which was located at the Canadian Sault.

"Yes, I recall on our last trip that you were licensed as both a river pilot and a lake pilot, Mr. Slaker."

"Oh sure.... I remember now.... you made this same trip last year. I make this run so many times I tend to forget. I do remember that your first mate was ill with the flu or something, and stayed in his cabin. In fact, I haven't seen him much on this trip either. Is he all right?"

"Oh yes. He spends much time with the crew. He says it is good for their morale."

Captain Tan knew that was a lie. The first mate, Chang Hai, had no use for the scurrilous crew members. Captain Tan knew that Chang Hai did not want to be observed too closely by the several Canadian and American pilots that were required to board the ship through the St. Lawrence Seaway System. He would make a brief appearance, and then become scarce until the next pilot boarded.

"And where is your home, Mr. Slaker?"

"I live right in Sault Ste. Marie.... on the American side. It's a lot smaller than the Canadian side. They say the population over there is about eighty thousand."

"Where is your home Captain.... Bangkok?"

"No. I spend much time there because it the *Badra's* home port. My home is in Singapore. I have no family. I have a small house there, and return whenever I have time off.... which is seldom when you are a sea captain."

The *Malaga Badra* sailed slowly through the narrow passage at Neebish Island and proceeded to the Sault. Its destination was the Algoma Steel Company at the Canadian Sault. The ship entered the MacArthur Lock, where it would be raised twenty-two feet to the level of Lake Superior. As the deck of the ship reached the exact level of the dock Pilot Rick Slaker stepped off.

"When will you be making another trip to the Soo, Captain Tan?"

"We will be back this season, I am certain, Mr. Slaker. I look forward to seeing you again." Captain Tan was a pleasant, friendly man, but Rick attributed his statement as Asian politeness rather than personal concern.

○

ON WEDNESDAY THE *MALAGA BADRA* WAS LOADED WITH Specialty Steel for delivery to Singapore. Singapore, in spite of its small area, had become a major Asian producer of computer chips. The colorful foreign freighter, with a bright red hull and four white derricks and booms, received its new American pilot and proceeded toward Lake Huron and eventually out through the St. Lawrence Seaway.

Now out in the Atlantic Ocean Captain Tan Wo Lin was at the helm with his first mate, Chang Hai. The last Canadian pilot had departed at Baie Comeau in Quebec at the mouth of the St. Lawrence.

"Did all go well with our mission, Mr. Chang?" Captain Tan stopped talking momentarily when he noticed the scratches on Chang Hai's face. He knew enough not to inquire about them.

He continued the conversation. "I have observed that our passenger has not appeared from her cabin in several days. I did not wish to discuss it with you when the American and Canadian pilots were still on board, since we did not officially list her as a passenger."

"She is no longer on board, my dear Captain. That is all you need to know." Chang Hai appeared to speak a little sarcastically, and surprisingly, with disrespect to his Captain.

"I discovered that she was not a reporter writing a story of her journey on an ocean freighter, as she claimed. I found a message she had prepared to send to Honolulu when we stopped at the Soo. The message indicated that she was spying on our operations. You can be assured that she is no longer spying on us."

Captain Tan Wo Lin was aware that his ship was being operated by an organization called the ODAM. He suspected that drugs and weapons were being smuggled into Detroit and Chicago from his cargo. His first mate, Chang Hai, seemed to be a major official in the organization. The Captain had been ordered to allow Chang Hai to have complete freedom on board.

Captain Tan had piloted the same ship since 1978, when it was owned by Fednav Marine in Quebec, and leased to a Bangkok shipping company. It was originally named the *Federal Orient*. In 1995, it was purchased by a front company for the ODAM group, and the name was changed to *Malaga Badra*. The Captain was just an employee and had no concern for the politics of his employer. He did gradually observe that the logistics of his shipments did not fit the normal pattern of a legitimate shipping company.

He was informed by management that Chang Hai had

authority over him in matters concerning the cargo, which was not normal for an ordinary first mate. The Captain also realized that he was expendable, should he interfere with the operation of his owners, and that his life might depend on remaining unconcerned.

Chang Hai asked, in his usual denigrating tone, "When are we due in Honolulu, my dear Captain?"

"We should arrive on June 27th, or early the next day. We are scheduled to remain there for three days before leaving for Singapore and on to Bangkok."

"Very good. I look forward to Honolulu. It is my favorite port."

5.

THURSDAY, JUNE 11

PROFESSOR BRADLEY KENDALL hopped in his 1990 auburn colored Mercedes Benz 300. It was a small version of the full size Mercedes to make the price more palatable. Brad had leased it for five years, and then purchased it at the end of the lease. It had over one hundred thousand miles on it, but still drove the same. He drove to the Lansing Airport on Thursday morning. He flew to Chicago's O'Hare Airport and then directly to Honolulu, arriving at 5:30 p.m. This was his seventh trip to Hawaii, but it was always a thrill. The sudden shift from the business-like practicality of the Midwest to the tropical leisure of Polynesian Hawaii was a culture shock more powerful than the effects of jet lag.

Brad rented a Buick LeSabre from Alamo and drove out onto Nimitz Highway. He had arranged to stay at the Royal Hawaiian this time. He had always gone as cheap as possible.... but this time he wanted to enjoy the famous Royal Hawaiian. Although Japanese-owned, it still had the local charm that one of the three oldest Hawaiian hotels should have. The Moana was the first hotel built in Waikiki, then came the Royal Hawaiian, and then the Halekulani. It bothered him a little that all three were now Japanese-owned. But he had to admit that they were maintained as first rate hotels. The Royal Hawaiian is one of the highest ranked hotels in the world for service.

SUNDAY, JUNE 14

BRAD WAITED UNTIL SUNDAY, WHEN HE HAD FINISHED HIS FRIDAY night and all day Saturday classes at Hickam Air Force Base, before calling George Tong at the Kahana Restaurant.

"George, I'm staying at the Royal Hawaiian. Where would you like to meet?"

"We had better meet tomorrow night.... at your hotel if you wish. Ingra Jensen has not yet reported in."

Brad said, "Let's meet at the House Without A Key over in the Polynesian Hotel.... at about eight o'clock. It's very private in that open lounge area."

The name of the House Without A Key was attributed to Ernest Hemingway, who was said to have loved the Polynesian Hotel. It was an informal patio lounge, serving unadorned, but tasty, sandwiches, snacks, and drinks, compared with the gourmet, and extravagant menus in the more formal dining rooms. The House Without A Key faced the ocean, with the familiar and classic profile of Diamond Head in the background. The featured entertainment was

Hokulani Kaleo, and the Polynesian Trio. She sang, and danced the slow Hawaiian style hula to music played by a trio of musicians. They were all older *kanes*, the name for the local Hawaiian men, Brad had learned from his many journeys to Honolulu.

Because of his repeated trips to Oahu, he considered himself a *kama'aina*, not merely a plain tourist. The locals were the native Hawaiians, and the *kama'ainas* were the non-native residents, which included a large assortment of Asian and Euro-Americans.

George was neatly dressed in a light beige suit with a plain matching tie. He was average height, and had an unmemorable face, for his ethnic makeup. Just what George wanted, an inconspicuous presence.

Brad imagined that the Asian-American women would be attracted to him, because he was pleasant looking. But George was too occupied for a personal life. He was constantly entangled in earth-shaking crises that were more urgent than women on his agenda.

"Good to see you, Bradley. It has been about a year, I suppose, since you were here last."

George knew exactly when Brad was last in Oahu to teach his class at the Kaneohe Marine Base. He was an amazingly perceptive man with a memory for details. He had to be, in order to challenge the world's most devious criminal minds. But George.... perhaps because he watched so many TV episodes of "Columbo".... did not like to advertise his extraordinary abilities.

George and Brad sat down at a table along the side of

the open patio. George ordered an ice tea, and Brad had to have his black coffee, with blue sugar, in spite of the tropical temperature. In early summer, when Brad's class was usually scheduled, the climate was quite comfortable. There was little rain, and the temperatures were in the lower 80's most of the day. The Trade Winds helped to vary the constancy of the heat, making it less humid.

As the dancer swayed alluringly in the moonlight to the soothing Hawaiian melodies, against the blue-green waters of the Pacific Ocean, and with the spectacular view of Diamond Head in the background, Brad was in a hypnotic trance. It would be hard to concentrate on George's serious matters under normal circumstances. But these were not normal circumstances.

"Ingra Jensen hasn't reported in for almost two weeks. It seems certain to me that she was the woman found dead at Mackinac," George concluded.

"I agree George. And we traced the *Malaga Badra* to the exact spot.... and at about the same time she would have been murdered. She must have been thrown off the ship. Or.... maybe not. If she was thrown off.... she couldn't have reached the shore at the Round Island Lighthouse. Maybe she jumped off.... swam to the nearest shore.... and then died from the stab wound. But.... why would someone try to kill her?"

Brad thought that George probably knew why. Or at least knew what she was doing on that ship. And he knew that George would reveal everything that he wanted Brad to know.... and nothing more. At this point Brad knew that George had just drafted him to serve on the team again. It must be something serious when one of the team members is murdered. He remembered the *Singapore Girl* who was murdered by an international terrorist group.

George explained, "Ingra boarded the *Malaga Badra* in Honolulu when it left here, back in April, for the mainland.

She was a reporter for the *Honolulu Star*. A perfect type for my mission. She had helped us on other.... less dangerous.... it turns out, assignments. So she agreed to work for us. She told the Captain, his name is Tan Wo Lin, that she wanted to write an article about life on a freighter, and picked their ship. Before she asked him, the *Star* deliberately picked their ship, at my request, for a feature article about her voyage.... so it would be hard for the Captain to turn her down."

"How did you get a newspaper to cooperate on the article without exposing the plan?"

"A retired feature writer, Eddie Sherman, who was often mentioned by Steve McGarrett in "Hawaii Five-O", helped me several times in exposing drug dealers. I could trust him to not reveal any connection between Ingra and the INS. He wrote the article for me, and the *Star* was happy to print his name on a featured guest article."

"Do people here in Hawaii know about the INS?" Brad wondered. "I mean the law enforcement authorities, like the state police, and the governor."

"The governor and a few others who are team members know about it. The general public thinks that the INS is just as it sounds, an Information Network System. If the name is ever exposed accidentally, we have established a dummy corporation that operates as an information system to distribute news to the media. So far we have not been discovered by the international criminals we are opposing."

"Thanks George, I wondered how you remained a secret to the underworld."

"Members like you and Sam know how important it is to remain a secret operation. I trust that they didn't try to get any information from Ingra before she was murdered."

Brad recalled, "I heard Oscar.... he's the Mackinac County medical examiner.... tell Reino.... you remember Reino, he's the local sheriff.... that there were some bruises on her body.... but nothing to indicate rape or a beating."

"That's a good sign. But I wonder why they had to kill her?" George was almost omniscient, but he didn't know that answer yet.

"Do you know who *they* are, George?"

"We have been following the trips made by the *Malaga Badra* since 1996, a year after it was purchased by a company owned by a group called the ODAM."

George continued, "We know that ODAM, which is probably an acronym for their organization, is a group of terrorists who hate the United States. They are planning a major attack somewhere in the Great Lakes area. We know because in the past year the *Malaga Badra* has made the same trip from Bangkok to Honolulu, then through the St. Lawrence system to either Detroit or Chicago. Then it picks up specialty steel at the Algoma plant in the Canadian Sault on the return trip, bound for an Asian port like Singapore, Hong Kong, or Bangkok."

"That sounds innocent enough." Living on the Straits, Brad was familiar with the international shipping patterns.

"True, but after each trip by the *Malaga Badra,* members of our INS in both Detroit and Chicago have reported an influx of military weapons in the hands of a secret group. They are either Communist fanatics or Neo-Nazis. We also have reports of drugs smuggled in at about the same time."

"Don't they check the *Malaga Badra* more closely at the customs entry points.... especially since you suspect it?"

"No," George replied. "I haven't reported it to the customs because I want to monitor every move they make.... so we can anticipate their strategy. If we stop one ship now, they'll just start a new approach."

"I get it. You'd have to start all over again, too. Sam Green didn't seem to know anything about the *Malaga Badra* when I saw him in Mackinaw."

"No, in Detroit they unloaded only a small shipment of furniture for a Hudson's downtown warehouse.... so I hadn't told Sam about the *Malaga Badra,* yet. He knows about ODAM and its mainland based groups, and monitors them for me. We're fortunate to have the regional FBI Director on our team. And he works well with you and Reino."

"I'll be flying back to Mackinaw tomorrow.... that's Tuesday.... and then back here to teach another weekend session on June 25th. The classes are at Hickam on Friday and Saturday as usual. What's our next move going to be, George?"

"The *Malaga Badra* will be in the Honolulu Harbor on Monday or Tuesday after your next classes at Hickam. This might be a dangerous assignment.... so you don't have to volunteer for it."

"You know better than that, George. I love a dangerous

assignment." Brad was definitely not a risk-taker.... but every man, even the most timid, has a small itch for adventure.... even an unimaginative, scholarly, accounting professor, like Brad. "What would you like me to do?"

"I want you to go to the Captain, his name is Tan Wo Lin, and ask for Ingra. Tell him that you are a friend.... make it any type you wish.... and that you were supposed to meet her when the ship returned to Honolulu. Find out how the Captain is going to explain her absence."

"That doesn't sound too dangerous, George."

"Not at that point. But.... you don't know where your questions will lead. Now.... I am going to leave and let you enjoy the rest of your time here. Call me when you arrive and get settled. Where will you be staying?'

"I have a reservation at the Royal Hawaiian again. I love it there."

"Good, we can meet here at the House Without A Key again if you wish.... it's only a short walk from the Royal Hawaiian, and I think you like the entertainment."

The two men shook hands and George departed. George was right. Brad liked Madelaine Kaleo. She was a friend of Alina Chin. Billy and Alina Chin were childhood friends of Brad's. Both of their families were living in Spartan Village at Michigan State University when the children were in grade school. Brad had a crush on Alina, which was really a sisterly affection. He didn't have a sister, so Alina filled the void. The Chin family moved back to the Big Island, where Billy and Alina spent the rest of their childhood.

When Brad was teaching at the Kaneohe Marine Base last year, Billy and Alina introduced him to Madelaine.

Alina arranged for them to go to the House Without A Key for entertainment. Madelaine Kaleo was an instructor of music and dance in the Fine Arts Department at the University of Hawaii. She loved to perform, and was frequently asked to fill in for local dancers.

When she was featured as a singer and dancer, she used her middle, Hawaiian name, Hokulani, instead of Madelaine. It was more realistic for the tourists. She stopped at Brad's table after finishing her last performance for the evening.

"Hello.... is it Mr. Kendall?"

Madelaine knew quite well that he was Dr. Bradley Kendall, that good-looking professor from the mainland. She liked him at their first meeting with Billy and Alina last year. She had noticed that he seemed rather shy with women.... she liked that for a change. Most men were far too aggressive to suit her.

The truth was that Brad was overwhelmed by sensitive and charming women. They were almost too good to be true. Women in general had, not just physical attributes, but innate qualities that men could not imitate. A kind of instinctive concern and caring that only a female can exude. And when a woman in his presence also had physical beauty, as Madelaine did, his respect became almost a veneration.

For some complex reason his unique assessment of women made him less vulnerable to the artificiality of the aggressive females who had pursued him. He was a pretty good catch. An unattached, reasonably young college professor, whose overall appearance would be attractive to most discerning women. He became very fussy about women.... perhaps too fussy. He just couldn't find the perfect one for him.

At the sound of Madelaine's voice Brad snapped out of his trance. "Oh Miss Kaleo.... I'm so pleased that you remembered me. It was about one year ago that I was here. Please call me Brad."

"I will call you Brad.... and you will call me Madelaine.... please. Alina and I have talked about you several times since you were here. She and Billy both think you are a special friend. How long are you here this time?"

"I have to return to Mackinaw City tomorrow, but I'll definitely be back for my next classes on the 25th.... I believe that's on a Thursday."

"Oh how wonderf...." Madelaine stopped abruptly in order to restrain her enthusiasm. She had a strange attraction to him. She didn't understand exactly why. Many men were enamored with her.... too many. She was glad that she. didn't have the same problem as the famous *Singapore Girl*, whose suitors, usually complete strangers, had been known to commit suicide when rejected for a date.

But.... as a Hawaiian beauty, she had many proposals for promiscuous romances, and for marriage. She too was perhaps too fussy, having an ambiguous image of the perfect man. And up to now none of her suitors had measured up to her expectations. They were either sex crazy or money hungry. So Brad's combination of timidity with women and confidence with men, captivated Madelaine's attention. She knew that she must be cautious with this complex man.

"Oh.... I mean that I am sorry that you have to leave beautiful Hawaii so soon, but I am happy that you will be returning to enjoy it again."

That was about as noncommittal a statement she could muster up. She really wanted to say hurry back, and come to see me again.

Brad helped her. "I am staying again at the Royal Hawaiian when I return next week. I wonder if you would have time to show me some of the more interesting sites on Oahu.... you know what I mean.... not just the popular tourist attractions."

Brad had seen much more of Oahu, Kauai, and the big Island, Hawaii, than the itinerant tourist, but this was a great excuse to be with Madelaine without making it sound like a formal date. He was not brazen enough to go that far.

He remembered that she wasn't married because of what Alina had said, but he didn't know if she had a boyfriend, or was engaged. After all she was a beautiful young woman. Brad had also figured from Alina's comments that she would be about his age, or maybe a year or two younger.

"I would be happy to. The regular dancer at the House Without A Key, who was one of my students at the University, and is now a good friend of mine, is expecting a baby, so I am filling in for her. It will be quite a while before she can return. So I will be dancing every night except Sunday. When you return you can find me here.... and we can decide which day will be best for you.... for both of us.... that is."

"Thank you Madelaine, that is very thoughtful of you."

Brad reached out to shake her hand, like a prudish professor would to a business acquaintance, and departed for his hotel room. It took all of Madelaine's self-control to restrain herself from giving Brad the customary Hawaiian embrace, and a kiss on each cheek. But she did! Restrain herself.... that is.

6.

TUESDAY, JUNE 16

 BRAD FLEW OUT OF THE HONOLULU AIRPORT DIRECTLY to Chicago's O'Hare. Then he flew to Lansing, arriving in the morning.

He was dying for a Bob Evans breakfast, with their famous biscuits and gravy. There was a new Bob Evans Restaurant at the intersection of Highways 69 and 27, north of Lansing. He had arranged to have Sam Green meet him there for breakfast. Brad ordered his biscuits and gravy, accompanied by two eggs, bacon, and.... instead of pancakes, he had the fried mush, smothered with warm maple syrup. It all sounded so good, Sam ordered the same.

"I never knew they had this fried mush. It sounds horrible.... but it's ver-ry good," Sam agreed.

"Most people don't seem to know about the fried mush. It's better than pancakes." Brad noted. He then proceeded to tell Sam what he had learned from George in Honolulu.

"It seems certain that the murdered woman is this Ingra Jensen. George wants me to find out what really happened to her.... when I go back next week."

Sam responded between bites of the mush. "George kept me informed about some of the things you mentioned. I knew about the terrorist group ODAM and their enclaves in Detroit and Chicago. I'm coming closer to identifying the Detroit leader. I don't know yet what their political identity is. They're anti-American.... either Nazi or Commie. I hope to find out soon."

Sam continued, "George supplied me with an undercover agent in the Detroit ODAM group. She's a former hippie, with a police record of arrest at Wayne State University campus in the early seventies. I'm sure she was able to penetrate the very tight group only because of her record. She gave me this skimpy but helpful information on Mr. D. That's our code name for him.... short for Mr. Detroit, naturally."

"How about Mr. C? That must be your code name for Mr. Chicago!" Brad jested between gulps of his beloved black coffee with blue sugar.

"Nothing yet. We'll work on him next. It'll be harder for me since my offices are in Michigan." Sam had offices in both Detroit and Lansing.

Sam finished his breakfast and became serious. "I have a surprise for you, Brad."

Brad also assumed a serious look. "We-ll?"

"A young woman named Jennie Burke and her friend.... Joyce something or other.... are spending this weekend in Mackinac. They will stay at the Best Western this Friday and Saturday night."

"Sooo?"

"The girl named Jennie has a long blonde pony tail, and dresses a little hippyish!"

"Oh.... Oh yes.... I see.... you mean she's the one who George told you about. Then what?"

"The friend knows absolutely nothing about Jennie's... umm.... special assignment. Jennie and her friend will have dinner at the Admiral's Table Restaurant at six-thirty. You and Reino are to casually become acquainted with them.... that shouldn't be too difficult.... and offer to show them the town. When her friend isn't looking you must let Jennie know where you live. She has a reason to contact you, without her friend becoming suspicious."

FRIDAY, JUNE 19

AFTER BRAD HAD EXPLAINED SAM'S INSTRUCTIONS TO REINO they made plans to have dinner at the Admiral's Table Restaurant at six-thirty. The two women were easy to spot.

Jennie had a blonde pony tail and wore a floor length baggy blue denim dress. She looked like a hippie all right. The other young woman, in contrast, looked like a modern business-woman. She was dressed in well-fitting slacks and a short blue jacket over a white blouse. She had short dark-brown hair right out of the beauty parlor.

The two men managed to end their meal at the right moment in order to walk to the cashier at the same time as the women. Brad deliberately bumped into the girl he assumed was Jennie's friend.

"Oops. I'm sorry. Haven't I met you before... Miss... ?"

"The name's Joyce. No.... I'm sure we've never met

before. We're from Dearborn, and I haven't been in Mackinac for years. This is my friend, Jennie." The name gave Brad the identification he needed.

"Would you like us to show you around? I am Brad, and this is Reino." Reino didn't wear his sheriff's uniform for the occasion.

"Well.... I don't mind. How about you, Jennie?" Joyce laughed. "They seem harmless. Don't you think?"

Jennie assented. "If we get a free guided tour, it's all right with me."

They walked to the entrance of the new Courtyards.

"The Courtyards just opened last year. Lots'a shops and restaurants. There's a movie theatre.... and live entertainment every night. Isn't that right, Brad? You see, I live in St. Ignace, so Brad probably knows Mackinaw better than I do," Reino humbly acknowledged.

"Well I wouldn't say that.... but Reino's right. The Courtyards is a nice addition to Mackinaw. Not everyone was pleased to see the quaint town expand.... at first.... that is. But then, they probably said the same about the addition of Epcot at Disney World in Orlando, when the Magic Kingdom was the only attraction there."

Both Jennie and Joyce enjoyed Teysen's Gift Shop, and Marshall's Fudge on the main street. They walked past Snookums, around the corner to Sandpiper, and finally over to the Fort Fudge Shop. After that the girls were tired and wanted to head back to the Best Western. During a time when Reino had Joyce's attention, Brad slipped Jennie a small piece of paper with the directions to his cottage. They said their polite good-byes, and the two men departed.

"Ya know Bradley," said Reino, "that Joyce was a good looker.... but I wasn't too crazy about that gal still livin' in the sixties. Do you think she's just puttin' on a front?"

"I know.... she was a little kookie. But.... she was still a sweet girl. I'm not sure if she's exaggerating for a purpose or not. I'm sure we'll find out before this escapade is over."

○

BRAD WAS SOUND ASLEEP. IT WAS TWO O'CLOCK IN THE MORN-ing. Someone was knocking loudly at the front door. Brad woke up.... threw on a robe, and went to the door. He put the porch light on. It was a warm summer night with a light drizzle. Standing on the porch was Jennie, looking wet and bedraggled.

"Sorry I had to do this. I had no choice. I don't want Joyce to suspect anything."

"Didn't she hear you leave the room?"

"We have separate rooms. Her brother is a construction foreman working on a huge casino hotel at Sault Ste. Marie. He drove down to stay with his sister tonight. So we took separate rooms.... lucky for me."

"How about some 7-Up.... or Coke?"

"Do you have some tea? I'd love some hot tea. It's a little cool and damp out tonight."

"Sure. It'll only take a minute."

Everyone seems to say something will only take a minute, when they know darn well it will take three or four.... or maybe more. Brad put a cup of water in the micro for three minutes. Then the tea bag had to steep for three more minutes. Then the tea had to cool for two more min-

utes. So it took at least eight minutes before Jennie actually drank some tea. Why didn't Brad just say. "It'll only take
eight minutes?" Because nobody does!

Jennie made herself comfortable sitting at the rare
Rittenhouse table in the main room of the cottage. The
Rittenhouse was a six-foot long table from an extinct
Cheboygan company that made rough-hewn maple furniture for the cottages that stretched along the northern
shores of the Great Lakes and the large inland lakes like
Mullet and Burt. The knotty pine table top was flat, but the
underside was round in the original shape of the logs. The
uniqueness of almost everything in the cottage, including
the century old spurs that Brad's grandfather wore when he
was a boy, passed right by Jennie, whose attention was on
more important things.

"I'm sure you're wondering if I really am living in the
past.... like my appearance indicates."

"Reino and I did wonder about it."

"Sam Green told you a little about me, I suppose. So you
know that I have to be convincing that I still believe the
way I did when I was arrested. I really don't like to dress
this way any more.... but I'm afraid to change."

"We both suspected that you could be doing just that.
What I don't know is why you are here now."

"Sam told you about Mr. D.... I assume. Well Mr. D is a
man named Jacque Kamel. He is an animal.... devious....
and very clever. He works with ODAM, those hate-America
fiends over in the Middle East.... or somewhere in Asia. I
think they move around. They are cooperating with

Saddam Hussein, and what's-is-name from Libya, and now with some Pakistani terrorists. At least that's what Jacque tells me. I became involved with him a long time ago.... before he was this horrible. He always trusted me."

Jennie sighed and went on. "I stopped seeing him for about ten years.... after the anti-war stuff. Then he located me about five years ago and gradually lured me into his group. When I realized that I didn't believe in his hate ideas anymore it was too late. If I tried to get out now, I would be eliminated in a minute."

Jennie drank some more tea to wet her dry mouth a bit and continued. "George, you know .... in Honolulu, somehow found out about me, and convinced me to work with Sam Green. I haven't been able to pass much information to Sam about Jacque. So that is why I am here. I can't take any chances in Detroit. It's too risky. I was able to pass a message to Sam that I would be going to Mackinaw City, and he arranged the rest."

"How did George ever find you from way over in Honolulu?" Brad wondered out loud.

"I guess he's some kind of a miracle man. His computers put all that information about my past together into a probability pattern. Apparently my more up-to-date personal actions, like what I subscribe to.... and my friends.... add up to a significant change in my political leanings. So George took a chance and contacted me secretly. I was happy to finally have a possible way to get out of my predicament. Although I'm far from out of it yet."

"Is that the only reason you came to Mackinaw?"

"No. This all started when Jacque ordered me to come here. He wants me to go to Mackinac Island and get maps and take pictures."

"Anything in particular?"

"Definitely. He asked me to get information on both the Mission Point Resort and the Grand Hotel. He wants pictures inside and outside of the buildings, and as many brochures as I can get. He wants the Governor's Summer Residence too."

"Do you know what for?"

"Not exactly. I suspect that ODAM is planning something big to take place in this area.... probably on Mackinac Island.... but I don't know what it might be."

"Okay, Jennie. You go about your business as planned. Reino and I will have no further contact with you. We don't want anyone to get suspicious. How about your friend Joyce.... does Jacque know about her?"

"Yes. I told Jacque that it would be more natural for me to act like a tourist with a friend along. He agreed. And Joyce thinks we're just having a fun vacation."

They were both getting sleepy. It finally dawned on Brad that Jennie was a beautiful person. The warmth of her personality embellished the beauty of her face. His intrinsic distaste for what her artificial appearance was designed to represent had obscured her elegance and grace. But at three in the morning those kind of thoughts were too complicated to analyze.... thought Brad.

7.

SATURDAY, JUNE 20

◆ JENNIE AND JOYCE EACH HAD A LADY-LIKE BREAKFAST at the Lighthouse Restaurant and caught the ten-thirty Arnold Catamaran. It was a sunny but cool morning. The water temperature is still quite cool in June, so on cool mornings the air was clear. This made the water in the Straits a glistening deep blue-green color, and created an optical illusion of making everything appear closer. It looked as if you could reach out and touch the Mackinac Bridge and the Grand Hotel.

The ferry boat skimmed in between the two lighthouses, the Round Island Lighthouse, and the one closer to Mackinac Island, now called the Round Island Passage Lighthouse, and aimed at the dock. The two girls were bubbling with excitement at the spectacular view of this unique Island. They walked directly to the Chamber of Commerce Building, directly across from the Arnold Lines' dock, where they received a pleasant smile from a lady whose name tag read "Betsy".

"Welcome to Mackinac Island. How may I help you?"

Jennie spoke up, "We want to see Mission Point and the Grand Hotel."

"And I want to see Ste. Anne's Church.... and...oh.... of course, the Fort," Joyce interjected with haste.

Betsy said, "If you walk straight down this street.... Huron Street, that way," she pointed to her left, "you will first pass Fort Mackinac. There is a park, called Marquette Park, in front of the Fort. Further down is Ste. Anne's Church, which dates back to 1874. Then past the Church is the old Mission Church.... oldest church building in Michigan.... and then the Mission Point Resort. You can't miss it. It was a college campus at one time.... in the 1950s and 60s. Here are some maps and brochures. This one shows the route I described for you."

"Should we see the Fort first?" Joyce asked.

"It's up to you. It may take the most time at the Fort because of the size. So use your own judgment."

They walked down Huron Street to the catholic church, where the friendly priest personally showed them inside. Then they walked to the Mission Point Resort. The Great Hall in the main lodge had an enormous, vaulted log ceiling.

A guide told the ladies that it was built by the Moral Re-Armament Association in the 1950s. Then it became a college, lasting only four years. The guide said that Rex Humbard, the TV evangelist, bought it in 1969, and it failed again as a college. Later.... the guide didn't know exactly when.... it became the Mission Point Resort.

Jennie discovered a tourist map in the lobby that showed the location of every main building in the Resort. "Joyce, I'd love to see the dorms and the rest. These old college buildings fascinate me."

"Go ahead Jenn.... if you don't mind, I'd rather sit in the lobby.... I'm pooped!"

Jennie walked all around the Resort buildings, inspecting every nook and cranny. She used her map to make notations from her inspection. Jacque should be satisfied with this.... she tried to convince herself.

"Let's go, Joyce... I'm anxious to see the Grand Hotel," Jennie exclaimed.

All rested up, Joyce tagged along with the bouncy ex-hippie. They walked back along Huron Street, past the park in front of Fort Mackinac. After peeking in at Benjamin's Gift Shop, and looking at the Pub's tempting menu, Joyce wanted to stop at the Island Bookstore to browse. She asked the attractive young lady who waited on them, "How do we get to the Grand Hotel from here?"

The obliging clerk answered. "Turn right at the next block up to Market Street. Then turn left past the Landing Gull, and a few other gift shops along the way to Cadotte Avenue. Then walk up the hill. You'll see it."

Jennie had a little trouble getting Joyce past the Landing Gull, with all its tempting gifts and keepsakes. As they breathlessly reached West Bluff Road at the top of the hill, the view was worth the effort. They each paid the five dollar fee to go inside the Grand Hotel, and to walk on the longest porch in the world.

Jennie examined the layout of the Grand Hotel as carefully as she could without appearing eccentric, obtaining any maps and visitor's guides that described the rooms and grounds. To her relief, there was an abundance of promotional literature that described every aspect of the tourist attractions on the Island.

Completely exhausted, the two friends left on the five o'clock ferry back to Mackinaw City. They were too tired to see the Fort. Each one said.... tomorrow.... maybe tomorrow. When they reached their rooms at the Best Western they both collapsed into their beds and dozed off for almost an hour. Joyce's brother had stayed overnight with her, and then returned to Sault Ste. Marie in the morning before the gals left for the Island.

Joyce woke up at six-thirty, combed her hair, straightened up a bit, and called Jennie's room.

"Is there any way we can get in touch with those two nice fellows we met yesterday? I kinda liked the one called Rhino.... or whatever."

"It was Reino, pronounced rain-o. Don't you know your Finnish culture? The UP is full of it."

"No, I'm just a city girl. Anyway I liked him."

"Then let's go to the new Chinese restaurant, Chee Peng. It's near the IGA grocery store. The other fellow, Bradley... said the food was good and he knows the owner. We can ask him."

Jennie didn't want to see the men again, but she didn't want to explain why to Joyce. The ladies were seated by a young waitress. They ordered Sweet and Sour Chicken and Egg Foo Yong. They both had the Egg Drop Soup and.... of course.... a pot of Chinese Jasmine Tea.

Joyce asked the waitress about Bradley and Reino. "The one called Bradley is a professor.... he lives here in Mackinaw, I think .... maybe just in the summer... and the other one, Reino, is from St. Ignace. Do you know either of them?"

The waitress said, "Oh yes.... I know Reino. He's the sheriff over across the bridge. He comes here a lot.... not only with the professor.... but with the local policemen. I don't know where the professor lives. My husband might know.... he and I are the owners.... but he had to go to Midland and Mt. Pleasant today."

Jennie wasn't anxious to pursue the search so she kept out of the conversation. Finally, Joyce gave up on her desire to find Reino. After dinner they walked over to the band shell by the water where a band was playing Sousa marches. They both swore that the silver haired director must be Sousa himself, reincarnated.

They walked along the shops on the main street for a while, and through the Courtyards to watch the light show. Finally exhausted they returned to their rooms for the night.

On Sunday morning they both slept in until check-out time. They had breakfast at the Pancake Chef and decided to drive home before the traffic got too heavy. It was Jennie's idea. She had accomplished her mission to her own satisfaction. She would never admit it to anyone, including herself.... but she really wanted to see that professor again.... although not with Joyce around.

For women who intuitively yearned for the perfect man, Bradley was irresistible. There was nothing spectacular about his personality or his looks. It was an inexplicable mystical anomaly. Although sometimes attracted to his physical appearance, shallow and brazen women interested only in sex had no continuing interest in him. He was not prudish, but it would become obvious that they had nothing in common.

What Jennie didn't imagine was that Brad had a similar feeling about her. His emotional side wanted to see her again, while his analytical side argued that it would be safer to wait. So Jennie and Joyce drove back to Dearborn without saying good-bye to the two mysterious men who had entered their lives.... and Joyce had no idea of the complex, bizarre, and exciting implications of their not so accidental meeting at the Admiral's Table Restaurant on Friday night.

8.

THURSDAY, JUNE 25

THE CLASSES AT HICKAM AIR FORCE BASE MET ON Friday night and all day Saturday for three weekends, separated by two weeks. This allowed the busy students, mainly pilots, time to study several chapters at a time, in order to prepare for the concentrated sessions. Only well organized and highly disciplined students could withstand such an intensive schedule, especially for Brad's course in Management Accounting. He found out from experience that the military provided the best training for such rigor.

The schedule meant that Brad had to fly back to Hawaii every two weeks, or stay on Oahu for five weeks. Last year he remained the full five weeks, giving him time to visit Kauai and the Big Island. He enjoyed seeing Kilauea as it was spouting out flames and lava. This year, after the first two-day session, he had reasons to return to the mainland.

He drove his senior citizen Mercedes 300 the two hundred and twenty miles to the Lansing Airport, where he boarded the United Express to Chicago, and from there, on to Honolulu. While teaching at Hickam he learned that the runways at the Honolulu International Airport were adjacent to those of Hickam Air Force Base. Some runways were used by both military and commercial airplanes.

As the plane circled for a landing it passed over Diamond Head, which looked entirely different from the air. It looked like any other crater from the top.... it was the side view from the ground that was the famous tourist attraction.

On the left, during the landing approach, Brad spotted the large pink building. His academic mentor and good friend, Professor Roy Nelson of the University of Hawaii, told him that the pink building was Tripler Army Hospital, where he had taught in 1988.

The main hospital building was impressive, high on the lush hillside above Pearl Harbor. Although not completed until shortly after World War II, it served as a military hospital for the wounded of the Korean and the Vietnam wars. It has continued to serve as a military hospital for the Pacific basin.

Walking from the plane to the main airport was like entering another world. The fragrance of the tropical flowers, the mist over the lush, green hills in the background, and the moist warm air gave one a heavenly feeling. Brad could almost hear Herve saying.... "da plane.... da plane...." And he wouldn't have been a bit surprised if Ricardo Montalban greeted him saying, "Welcome to Fantasy Island."

Snapping out of his delightful trance Brad observed the treatment given to an organized tour group. They were greeted by beautiful Hawaiian girls in their grass skirts, who tossed their homemade leis over the heads of the tourists. After receiving a lei around his neck, a kiss on each cheek, and a few sensual twists of the hips by a bare-footed, curvaceous Tahitian beauty one old man walked off in a heavenly trance that probably lasted his entire Hawaiian tour.

Brad had made this trip enough to know the ropes. He hopped an Alamo bus, which took him six or seven blocks to the rental lot. He stood in line for twenty minutes while some inexperienced tourists hemmed and hawed about some facet of the rental car. He finally drove out with his choice, a four-door Buick LeSabre. It was white, which seemed to be the favorite rental color in Hawaii. It seemed that every older Japanese tourist was driving a white Towne Car.

Brad always wondered why they didn't pass a law to allow only electric cars in the Hawaiian Islands. It is only about ninety miles around Oahu. Who needs a car that goes eighty miles per hour, and can go four-hundred miles on one tank of gas? He drove down Nimitz Highway to Ala Moana Boulevard, which merged into Kalakaua Avenue. It was his favorite drive, because it took him along the water, through downtown Honolulu, past Ward Warehouse, which had some of his favorite restaurants, the Aloha Tower, Fort DeRussy, and into Waikiki. His destination was the historic Royal Hawaiian Hotel.

O

HIS UNEXPECTED FANCY FOR JENNIE HAD FILLED THE RESERVED space he allowed in his agenda for amorous thoughts. His rigorous analytical approach to time-consuming priorities in his life placed a limit on ambiguous concepts like romance.

His emotional response to how an enticing girl might affect him was undefined. He was subconsciously afraid to think of what a girl like Madelaine would do to him. She was not merely enticing, she was a voluptuous tornado of temptation.

Brad registered at the Royal Hawaiian requesting an ocean view room. Phooey on the fortune it cost him.... he bravely decided. The university paid him for teaching the course, plus a flat allowance for expenses. If they didn't limit the expense allowance, a visiting professor could spend a fortune, like Brad did for an ocean view room at the Royal Hawaiian. So Brad would have to pay the excess over the allowance. The allowance for a standard hotel room was far below the tab that Brad would pay for this luxurious room.

The other times he had taught this same course.... in Hawaii; Jacksonville, Florida; and in Charleston, South Carolina.... he always skimped on his costs. And the stereotyped cheapskate accounting professor was a master at frugality. This time, for some reason, Brad just wanted to splurge. After all, he didn't rent the mammoth Towne Car.... and he didn't fly first class. So a little splurge wouldn't hurt.... he rationalized.

Brad was getting hungry. I'll go to the Yum Yum Tree he decided. There's one close by in the Ward Centre.... or is it the Ward Warehouse? Oh.... it doesn't matter. It's in one of them. I feel a little tired. I'll just lie down for a few minutes.... he thought.

When you arrive in Honolulu at five-thirty in the late afternoon, pick up your luggage, rent a car, drive to the hotel, check in, and finally get to your room it is probably eight or nine o'clock in the evening. You think you're hungry, so you get spruced up ready to go out to eat. Then you feel tired.... why?.... because now it is between two and three in the morning in Michigan time. And your body is still living on Michigan time, not Hawaiian time. So you lie down.... just for a few minutes.... naturally. Boom! You fall asleep. When you wake up.... what a shock!

Brad woke up at eight o'clock on Friday morning. His class at Hickam didn't start until six that night, so he had plenty of time. He was fully prepared for the class because he had written the text, and knew the scheduled assignments thoroughly. He always perused the material before each class, even if he knew it well, so that he would be smooth in his delivery. By nine o'clock hunger pangs were nudging Brad.

For breakfast he loved the Kahana because they had the tastiest pancakes, with a fried egg on top, and two slices of bacon. The Kahana was his favorite restaurant because you could sit by the window and watch the giant goldfish. They were actually carp, swimming all around and underneath the dining room. There was a picturesque waterfall and Bonsai trees in the background. George Tong was the owner of the Kahana Hotel and Restaurant, but Brad went there for the food this time, not to see George. He would get in touch with him after his classes were over.

SATURDAY, JUNE 27

BRAD WAS RELIEVED WHEN HIS SATURDAY SESSION WAS OVER. IT started at eight and ended at five, with a one-hour lunch break. It was a grueling day for him and for the students. He gave four half-hour quizzes during that eight-hour session. Even these highly disciplined military personnel were exhausted at the end of the day. It was the thought of having dinner at the House Without A Key, and watching Madelaine dance, analogous to his dessert, that kept him alert.

He returned to his room and took a short nap. He woke up at seven and dressed casually, in beige summer slacks with a short-sleeved, button-down shirt with epaulettes. He didn't like the baggy, sloppy look of the yuppies. He sat at a table near the rear of the room where it was not crowded. At her next break Madelaine routinely disappeared to her dressing room. A few minutes later she emerged and sat down at Brad's table.

"Professor.... it is so nice to see you again." Madelaine sounded sincerely happy to see him..

"Remember Madelaine.... my first name is Brad. It must be hard to remember names. You meet so many people."

"I do meet many people.... but not like you. I did remember your name, Professor Bradley Kendall.... I just didn't want to appear too eager to let you know that I remembered. There.... I said it. I confessed!"

"Wow! And did you remember that you promised to show me around Oahu?"

"Yes, I did. I don't have to dance on Sunday.... tomorrow night. Is that a good time for you?"

Brad was pleased that she would be free so soon. "Great. I have a rental car and will pick you up at your home. By the way, I don't know where you live."

"I live near Billy and Alina in Waimanalo. Do you know how to get there?"

"I sure do. I've been to Billy's house several times."

She scribbled down an address on Laumilo Street for him. Brad could never forget that the drive along the ocean from Waikiki to Waimanalo had some of the most beautiful scenery in the world.

"Oh dear.... there's my cue from Ben. I'd better go." Ben Shirakawa was the leader of the three-piece Hawaiian band that accompanied Madelaine.

Brad said, "I'm leaving now, too. I'll pick you up at eleven. Is that all right?" She turned as she was heading for the stage, and eagerly waved her agreement.

On Sunday morning Brad drove to the Kalanianaole Highway toward Hawaii Kai. Not being able to pronounce Kalanianaole properly, he called it the Kalani Way. He drove up a long hill to Koko Crater, passing the entrance to the Underwater State Park at Hanauma Bay. The view from there to Waimanalo had to be one of the most beautiful anywhere. At the top of Makapu'u Point you can see all the way from Rabbit Island to Kailua Bay, with the lush Koolau Mountains in the background. Along this shore is where many of the scenes from "Magnum P.I." took place.

The town of Waimanalo is strictly Hawaiian, undiscovered by tourists. Next to Waimanalo is Bellow's Air Force Base, no longer fully operating. Only the locals and the kama'ainas went to Waimanalo Beach and Bellows

Beachpark. Laumilo Street was along the ocean where the property values were sky high. Even if the houses were not fancy, the value was in the eighty-foot ocean front lot.

Madelaine had inherited her small beach house from her Grandmother, Leilani Kaumeheiwa, who was one of the original members of the *tutu* movement in Hawaii. The *tutu's* were the elderly purebred Hawaiian women, most of them grandmothers, who volunteered to teach the young school children the language and customs of the Hawaiian people. Madelaine frequently assisted her grandmother in the program, until she died in 1985. Madelaine taught them the dances, while her grandmother taught them the chants.

Madelaine was ready when Brad knocked. He was stunned as she appeared in her beautiful muu'muu and homemade lei. She was the classic Polynesian hula dancer depicted on the tourist brochures, except that she was real.

They drove from Waimanalo to Kailua and then along Brad's favorite Kaneohe Bay Drive. They drove past the Kaneohe Marine Base where Brad taught last year. He thoroughly enjoyed his class at Kaneohe. The marines escorted him up to the Ulupau Crater, where he saw the Penn Battery and the home of the Red-Footed Booby Colony. The tourists never saw these attractions.

Penn Battery was the big gun turret from the sunken battleship, *Arizona*. It was taken off the top deck after the bombing, and barged over to the Windward side of Oahu. There it was buried three stories deep into the Ulupau crater wall, with the guns facing toward the ocean. It was accompanied by one machine gun nest a few hundred yards away, awaiting the invasion.... which never came.

Years later the Red-Footed Boobies made that crater wall their home.

They stopped at the Crouching Lion, a hillside restaurant named, like Diamond Head, after the profile seen in the distance by the motorists driving along the ocean. Madelaine suggested their unusual quiche lorraine. Brad didn't believe in silly cliches like, "Real men don't eat quiche!" He loved quiche!

The drive around Oahu was a ninety-mile circle. They continued northward to the little town of Laie where Brigham Young University's Hawaiian campus and the Mormon Tabernacle were located. One of the most popular tourist attractions in Hawaii was the popular Polynesian Cultural Center. It was operated by the University, with only native Polynesians from Hawaii, Fiji, Tonga, the Marquesas, New Zealand, Tahiti and Samoa doing the entertaining. Since it would take all day to see everything, Brad, who had already visited the University and the environs by invitation from one of his professor friends, opted to move on.

The road circled around the top of the Island past the Kahuku Sugar Mill, the Turtle Bay Hilton, and Sunset Beach, where the master surfers displayed their bravery.

They then drove southward past Kole Kole Pass, where the Japanese Mitsubishi bombers and Zeros nefariously slithered into U.S. territory and headed straight for Pearl Harbor.

They stopped at the Dole Pineapple Visitor's Center for a free sample of pineapple. And from there it was all downhill to Pearl City and Honolulu. Brad drove over the

Likelike Highway back to Kaneohe. As soon as he saw the highway sign for the Likelike Highway he couldn't resist telling Madelaine his corny rhyme, which came about when he learned that Likelike was pronounced licky licky, and that wicky wicky meant fast or quickly in Hawaiian.

He spurted out, "The tutu's wore their muu'muu's as they drove wicky wicky over the Likelike." She laughed.... probably out of politeness.

They were both exhausted by the time they returned to Waimanalo and Madelaine's quaint little beach house. She invited him in for a drink. He asked for pineapple juice, which was one of her choices.

"That was so much fun," Madelaine said. "I hope you enjoyed it too."

"I sure did." Brad relaxed in a comfortable white wicker chair, and looked out at the pacifying Pacific Ocean, making him realize how the ocean may have gotten its name.

Madelaine went into her bedroom, combed her long silken black hair out, and took off her conservative, long muu'muu. She put on a skimpy short flowered muu'muu, which revealed more of her curvaceous figure than Brad was prepared for at the moment. Nothing could shock Brad's academic trained, objective, composure.... but.... he had no control over his innate masculine hormones, which erupted when she pranced out in her bare feet. Romantic thoughts dominated him for a change.

"Ahhh..... Madelaine.... I just wondered.... am I taking you away from your..... umm.... time with other friends.... I mean.... like girlfriends..... or ahhh..... maybe boyfriends?" It was Brad's clumsy attempt to unravel the mystery of

Madelaine's love life. She was just too darn scrumptious not to have boy friends.

She toyed with him. "I have lots of boyfriends."

That's no answer he thought. I'll try again. "Well I don't like to interfere in..... you know.... your private life. If I am embarrassing you by being here.... well, I wouldn't want to...."

"You're not embarrassing me. I'm a big girl now. I live alone. I have lots of men here."

Boom! She has lots of men in her house. "You mean.... lots of men?"

"Sure my brother..... my father.... even my minister visits me once in a while." She giggled.

"Phew.... I was worried for a minute." Brad was an absolute bumbler with women.

But that only made him more adorable to Madelaine. He was showing honest romantic feelings toward her, she sensed. She also sensed that prancing and wiggling around in her revealing muu'muu might be too brazen and scare him off.... so she sat down.

Since Brad didn't get a warning of any sort, he assumed that she wasn't tied to anyone. He was too proud to come right out and ask her, so he just stopped tossing out his verbal bait. And Madelaine knew that the more mysterious her love life remained, the more tempting she would be to him. So she offered no more voluntary personal information.

"Madelaine.... thank you for such a lovely day. I think we're both ready for bed.... I mean.... that is, I didn't mean.... oh, you know what I meant. If you don't mind, I would like to see you again before I leave. And I'm not going back between classes this time. So I'll be here for twelve days, with no plans, before the last two sessions begin."

"Of course I don't mind. I'll be at the Polynesian every night starting Monday. Please come to see me whenever you want to." That was about as forward as she dared to go with this intricate fellow. She was thrilled at the prospect of his staying that long.... with no plans! She would make sure that he had plans to see her. He just didn't know about them, yet!

Brad had no idea what George's plans for him would fully entail. Just a friendly little visit to a foreign ship. No problem.... he innocently thought! He would have shuddered with apprehension if he knew what was in store for him.

On Monday morning Brad called George at the Kahana. "I am free to go to work now, George. My classes are over for this session."

"Very good, Bradley. The *Malaga Badra* is docked at the Honolulu Harbor. You know what to do. Ask Captain Tan about Ingra Jensen. Make up any story you wish, but memorize the details of her story to them. I'll review it again for you."

George continued, "She was actually a reporter for the *Honolulu Star*. She told Captain Tan that she wanted to write an article about life on a freighter. Remember that, at my request, the *Star* had deliberately picked his ship for a feature article about her voyage."

"Thanks George. I remembered most of it. I'll say that I work with her, and just play it by ear from there."

9.

MONDAY, JUNE 29

THE MALAGA BADRA HAD ARRIVED AT THE HONOLULU harbor on Saturday. It was scheduled to leave on Tuesday at noon. Brad arrived at the docks in the early afternoon on Monday. He walked up the steps beside the historic Aloha Tower to the deck level. He approached an apparent crewman on the deck of the *Malaga Badra*.

"Is the captain available, officer?" Brad knew he was not an officer by his uniform and general appearance, but to flatter was to gain cooperation.... he learned from experience.

"E'ze in the 'elm, sir." The combination of Scottish and Cockney accent gave a clue as to where this bloke had come from. Probably an Aussie, originating from London. "Ye're free to go up there, mate."

Brad climbed the stairwells to the pilothouse and entered the open doorway. "Are you the captain, sir?"

"Yes, I am Captain Tan. How may I help you, mister.... ?"

"It's...." Brad hesitated. He had just one second to make an important decision. Should he make up a new name, or give his real name. If he used a fictitious name, and had to show identification, he would be caught in a lie. If he gave his real name he would be lying about other things. So he blurted out in an instant.

"It's Brad Kendall. I'm a reporter for the *Honolulu Star*. I'm here to find Ingra Jensen. She was supposed to call me when she got back from her trip to the Great Lakes on your ship. We're all waiting for her story. But she hasn't called me.... or anyone else at the *Star*. Do you know where she is? She's my girlfriend, too."

The first mate, Chang Hai, took over immediately as Captain Tan turned his eyes toward him. Brad was amused at how much Chang Hai looked like Peter Lorre.... or was it the fictional Wo Fat in "Hawaii Five-O"?

"Mr..... was it.... Kandell....?" He began.

"That's close enough." Brad didn't want to waste time on pronunciation.

"I am First Mate Chang Hai. The young lady was on board for a long time. She seemed to enjoy every minute. I say that because she mentioned it to me many times. When we arrived in Chicago.... let me see.... when would that have been, Captain Tan?"

Captain Tan looked at some papers. "It was on May 28th. We remained in Chicago for three days."

Chang Hai continued, "I recall that the young lady told both me and the Captain that she would visit a relative who lived in Western Springs, apparently a suburb of Chicago. We both reminded her that the ship would depart sometime after midnight on Monday morning, in order to adhere to our schedule. She was told to be on board by eight o'clock Sunday night. Is that not correct, Captain Tan?"

"Yes.... exactly as I recall." The good captain would not even think of changing one word.

Chang Hai continued, "At eight o'clock she did not return. She did not board the ship. She did not tell us anything about her relative. There were too many Jensens in the telephone book. And there was no certainty that the relative had the same surname."

Chang Hai seemed much too sympathetic to be believed by Brad, whose discernment sized him up as a cold, callous egotist. He couldn't imagine Chang Hai bothering to look in the telephone book, except for the nearest bawdy house.

"So you sailed off as scheduled. Did you see her anywhere again?"

"No. That was the last we heard of her," Chang Hai concluded his story.

"Captain Tan. Where is your next port?" Brad asked.

"Singapore. We depart tomorrow for Singapore, and then to Bangkok. We will be in the Singapore Harbour for four days."

Brad pursued his inquisitiveness. "How long does it take to sail from here to Singapore?"

"It will take six or seven days depending on the weather and the sea."

Brad's imagination was working overtime to invent an irresistible request.

"The *Honolulu Star* has promoted this story to the point that the management, my bosses, will be very embarrassed if it doesn't come out soon. I was more than a friend to Ingra. We were engaged. Wherever she is.... or whatever happened.... I don't want her to be hurt. I don't want her to lose her job.... assuming she's still all right."

Brad then took a big step.... more like a leap for him. "Would you let me go with you to Singapore? I could write the story from my experiences on the ship during the six or seven days. I could get off in Singapore.... fly back to Honolulu.... and then turn the story in."

The Captain turned to Chang Hai with a noncommittal look. Surprisingly to Captain Tan, Chang Hai said, "I don't see any reason why not. Do you Captain?"

Captain Tan would not contradict Chang Hai, and said, "No. Except that we cannot prepare all the paperwork in time. If we do not officially list you as a passenger we can omit the paperwork. But.... you must not tell anyone. When you enter the Singapore immigration you will need a passport. Do you have one?"

"Yes. I have a current passport. Thank you both. When should I board?"

Captain Tan looked at his watch.... probably a reflexive action since it had nothing to do with the answer. "Be here tomorrow at ten.... promptly. We will leave the harbor at noon. Have enough clothes, but you don't need much on a ship. You can't go to a restaurant or a nightclub."

Brad was pleased to note a sense of humor from Captain Tan. He said, "I'll be here at ten, with my belongings. I'll need my desktop computer, and a camera. Is that all right, Captain?" He wanted the captain to answer, instead of Chang Hai, who seemed to be making all the decisions.

Captain Tan hesitated before he answered, allowing Chang Hai time to say no if he wished. With no response from Chang Hai he said, "Yes, it is perfectly all right."

O

BRAD DROVE STRAIGHT TO THE ROYAL HAWAIIAN. HE MADE A couple of wrong turns, each time stopping the car, and waiting for a few minutes. He wanted to make sure that they didn't suspect him of something. He called George at the Kahana, telling him the whole story.

"Well, Mr. Bradley Kendall. You've jumped in with both feet now." George coined an Americanism probably picked up from an old movie. "Be very careful. As soon as you get to Singapore, contact me, and I will arrange for your flight back. I will have an INS member in Singapore watch for you in case you need any help. Go to the Carleton Hotel. I'll reserve a room for you."

"Thank you, George. You'll hear from me in about a week. Captain Tan said he is scheduled to arrive in Singapore on about July seventh. I'm going to find out what really happened to Ingra if it kills me.... whoops.... I shouldn't have said that. I mean I'll do all I can to find out."

That night at eight o'clock Brad walked the short distance from the Royal Hawaiian to the Polynesian Hotel. He meandered over to the House Without A Key and found a table near the back. At her next break Madelaine hurried over to see Brad. The joy in her face was obvious.

"Please sit down for a minute, Madelaine." Brad sounded too serious. She instinctively frowned.

"I have to leave Hawaii tomorrow.... for at least a week.

I didn't know on Sunday when I last saw you." He wanted to say that he was sorry.... but that would be presumptuous. Why would he assume that she would be disappointed?

Madelaine skillfully restored her composure, which was just about to expose her disappointment. "I hope you have a safe trip. May I ask where you are going?"

"Singapore. I'll be there one week. When I get back .... do you mind if I come to see you again?"

"Oh no. I would like you to come again. I am so sorry that you can't.... " Madelaine stopped. She didn't want to expose her more fervent desires. And.... she didn't want to discourage him.

"There's Ben waving me back to the front. Remember, I'll be here when you get back. And.... I do look forward to seeing you again."

10.

THE *MALAGA BADRA* LEFT HONOLULU HARBOR ON schedule. Professor Bradley Kendall was on board and was assigned the same stateroom that Ingra had. All of her belongings were gone. Brad searched everywhere carefully, without any luck. The weather was calm for the first five days. The ship was right on schedule.

Captain Tan Wo Lin and Chang Hai were in the pilothouse. "What do think of our guest, Mr. Chang? Do you suspect that he is with the same group of spies as that woman? You did dispose of her, did you not?"

"Let us continue to say, my dear Captain that she disappeared of her own volition. I do not wish to claim any assistance in her departure from our good ship."

Chang Hai continued, "As for our guest. I will not trust him until he departs from our ship at Singapore without incident. He appears far too sophisticated to be a reporter of his reputed stature. He is hiding something.... I am certain."

Captain Tan Wo Lin said, "There is nothing he can learn about the woman's departure from us. So we have nothing to fear. I don't even know what happened to her. Although I do know that she didn't depart at Chicago in the manner you described to our guest. She was here on the bridge on the evening before we passed the Mackinac Bridge. That was the last time I saw her."

"But you would tell that to no one.... I presume.... my dear Captain."

"You may be assured that I will not.... my dear first mate." This time the Captain used a sarcastic tone.

○

IN THE MIDDLE OF THE FIFTH NIGHT AT SEA, BRAD WAS AWAKened by a quiet knock. He opened the door a crack. The man stayed behind the door and whispered.

"Keep it roight there, mate. Oi want to tell ya. A friend a mine saw the first mate toss that lai'dy into the drink."

Brad recognized the mixed brogue as that of the seaman he first met on the deck in Honolulu.

"Do you know why?"

"No.... mate. 'E just saw it.... that's all 'e tol me. 'E recognized the first mate, Chang, for shure. 'E said Chang drove a knife inta the lassie's back. Then o'er the side she goes."

Before Brad could say thank you, the man was gone. He had trouble sleeping the rest of the night. During the next day Brad, who was free to walk around the main deck, purposely looked for the seaman. Not seeing him around anywhere, Brad assumed that he probably worked somewhere below deck.

Later that day, the sixth day at sea, the Communications Officer entered the Bridge and handed Captain Tan a communication. Captain Tan dismissed him, and read the message carefully. He called for Chang Hai, who appeared a few minutes later.

He handed the communication to Chang. "This will verify who our cruise guest really is. His publications are those of an experienced professor, not a junior reporter."

Chang Hai read the message slowly, and mumbled to himself, "I see.... I see...."

He turned to the Captain and said, "I will take care of this. You will not be involved. All you need to know is that our voyager will be going all the way to Bangkok with us.

There the ODAM will take charge. He must be a spy. They know how to deal with spies. They will make him talk."

That night there was a knock on Brad's door again. He ho-hummed and yawned, to wake up from a deep sleep. Expecting his Cockney friend, he opened the door wide this time. He wanted to see him and get more information if possible.

Two men dressed in black sweaters, with hoods over their heads, swooped in and grabbed Brad. One injected him with something. They taped his mouth and held him down until he lost consciousness.

TUESDAY, JULY 7

THE *MALAGA BADRA* SAILED INTO SINGAPORE HARBOUR, THE second busiest harbor in the world, on Tuesday morning.

The spacious harbor was dotted with foreign freighters, anchored in every available space. One could see more foreign freighters in Singapore Harbour in one glance than most Americans would see in a lifetime.

The *Malaga Badra* was given an anchor site in Marina Bay, at the mouth of the Singapore River. It was not far from the famous Merlion statue, a mythical symbol of a lion and a fish. The lion stands for Singapura, meaning Lion City.

The two seamen were in First Mate Chang Hai's cabin. "We put him in the starboard hold with the cargo for Bangkok, sir. That was six hours ago. He hasn't had any food or water, and he should be awake by now."

Chang Hai said in his authoritative tone, "Good work.... here is your bonus." He handed them each one hundred dollars in U.S. currency.

"Give him some water.... no food.... yet. I will take care of the food. You have done your part for now."

Brad woke up, shocked to find himself bound and gagged. He was in complete darkness. Every part of his body seemed to ache, and his mouth was dry. It was painful to swallow. What an idiot, he accused himself. Why did I do such a stupid thing? He realized that his probable plight was to be thrown overboard.... or worse.

One of the seamen entered the hold, temporarily ending the darkness. "Here's some water. Drink, but don't ask any questions. I have orders not to answer."

Brad was thankful for the water enough to obey the seaman's command. He didn't say a word, knowing that it would be useless to get any information from him. An hour later he fell asleep, still affected by the drug.

Shortly after midnight he woke up. Someone was shaking him. A flashlight was on. His feet were already untied, and the man was untying his hands. The gag was still on.

"Ere now mate. Before I take yer gag off.... I'm yer friend. No noise.... not a peep.... ya 'ear.... nary a peep!"

He took the gag off, put a finger to his lips, and helped Brad to stand up.

"Foller me mate.... an do exactly as yer told."

The two men climbed to the main deck. There was a full moon. No need for the flashlight up on deck. The Cockney led Brad to a Jacob's ladder on the starboard side. They climbed down to a rowboat and silently rowed away. Being anchored so close to the land, it was only a short distance to a long freight dock. After tying up the rowboat, they ran down the dock. Brad was wobbly, but managed to keep up with his nebulous benefactor.

A Silver Grey Mercedes Benz 450 was waiting at the street end of the dock. The driver knew to go to the Carleton Hotel on Bras Basah Road.

"How can I thank you?" Brad said to the Cockney. "You saved my life. They were going to kill me.... I'm sure. I don't even know your name.... to thank you."

"It's Ian Gillespie. Scottish.... but I was brought up in ol' London town. An' don't thank me. It's George ya want ta thank. E' arranged everything."

"I might have known. But.... how did you manage to get on the crew of the *Malaga Badra?*"

"In 'onolulu one of the crew members ate at the Kahana Restaurant. George made sure e' got sick.... food pois'nin'. Then I shows up on the dock, just in the roight place, at the roight time. Even 'is eye'-ness, Mr. Chang, couldn't resist me."

Brad immediately felt the hot, humid night air of Singapore, which was only one degree north of the equator, and had almost no seasonal variation. It was seventy degrees even at night. They traveled through downtown Singapore, passing Bugis Street, the former transvestite area, now a shopping area for tourists, to the Carleton Hotel. The modern Carleton looked down on the elegant and luxurious Raffles Hotel. The celebrated haven for the rich and famous was named after Sir Stamford Raffles. He transformed an insignificant island into a British Territory in 1819, which became the modern and influential Singapore of today.

As the Mercedes pulled into the circular drive at the Carleton, Ian said, "By the waiy, this is 'arry. E's one of Georgy's boys, too."

Brad remembered what George had said. One of the INS members from Singapore will be available to help if needed. And 'arry.... Harry, that is.... was needed all right!

Harry.... like almost every Singaporean.... spoke excellent English.... but, with the typical British-Asian accent. Some were difficult to understand.... but not Harry.

At their departure, Ian said, "Yer won't see me again, mate. I 'ave to disappear fast.... or me goose is cooked. By now, me mission on the ship mus' be obvious ta 'is eye'-ness, Mr. Chang. You got 'arry 'ere ta lean on if ya need 'im."

"I owe you a lot Ian. I'll never forget what you did. Thank you!"

Harry said, "I know it is just after three in the morning....

but the clerk at the desk is expecting you. He thinks you were on a delayed flight.... which happens frequently. Remember now.... your plane leaves tomorrow at two-thirty for Honolulu. Here are your tickets and instructions from George. My unlisted number, only used by George and INS members, is there if you need it tomorrow. Destroy it as soon as you arrive in Honolulu safely. Any questions?"

"No. Thanks 'arry.... sorry.... I mean Harry. I won't call on you unless there's a serious problem."

The Mercedes drove off in the middle of the night, and poor old Brad felt safe at last. He registered without a hitch, and flopped into a spacious bed in the classy Carleton Hotel room.

THURSDAY, JULY 9

THE NEXT DAY BRAD BOARDED A TAXI FOR THE CHANGI INTERnational Airport. It was one of the most beautiful, and certainly the most efficient airports he had ever seen. There were tropical orchids decorating some of the waiting areas, and it was sparkling clean throughout.

He was surprised that all taxis charged the same fare, $15.00 in Singapore currency.... just slightly more than $10.00 in U.S. currency, and no tip was expected.

The immigration officials were polite, but not talkative. Americans have a reputation of being so garrulous, and some so obnoxious, that they are easily recognized in foreign countries. In Asia, however, Brad noticed that there were very few American tourists. Singapore was popular with the Australians, some whom Brad observed were just as boisterous as the Ugly American.

George had made his reservation on a Singapore International Airlines (SIA) flight to Honolulu. He knew how Brad felt about the famous Singapore Girl, the SIA stewardess. Each petite, thin Singapore Girl wore a full-length exquisite print, Mandarin style dress. The round face, silken black hair and eyebrows, over the slightly slanted sparkling dark-brown eyes resembled that of a painted oriental doll.

Brad was mesmerized by them. They didn't seem real .... until one actually talked to him. Then he was so awed by her physical presence that he didn't hear what she said. It was either do you wish coffee.... or would you like a pillow. Nothing was important enough to penetrate his hypnotic, trance-like admiration of this icon of Asian beauty.

During the long flight he dozed off. He dreamed that the Singapore Girls were really wind-up dolls. When one would wind down she would come only to him. He would reach around to the middle of her back and turn the wind-up key.

She would thank him with a little kiss on the forehead, and continue serving the passengers.

The next time he woke up from dozing off, the plane was circling for a landing at the Honolulu International Airport. The familiar sight of Honolulu, Waikiki, Diamond Head, and the Koolau Mountains snapped him out of his world of dreams. The memory of his not too pleasant voyage on the *Malaga Badra* placed him back into the real world.

11.

PROFESSOR BRADLEY KENDALL ARRIVED IN HONOLULU on Thursday, July 9th, thanking God for his safe return. He said good-bye to the Singapore Girls he had befriended on the flight. He found himself instinctively looking at the middle of their backs for the key.

According to the time, the flight went so fast that he landed in Honolulu before he departed from Singapore, since he left at two-thirty p.m., and arrived at noon of the same day. His romantic side wanted to believe that his fanciful contemplation of the Singapore Girls on the plane made time stand still. But that wouldn't explain how time went backwards.

His objective side was aware that the plane had crossed over the International Date Line, and that the combination of flight time, and distance time going east did not equal the twenty-four hours gained by crossing the Date Line. That would explain how time went backwards.

He rented a Buick LeSabre, again from Alamo, and drove straight to the Royal Hawaiian Hotel. There he spent the rest of the day relaxing in the pool and on the beach. After his ordeal he was too exhausted to want to see Madelaine right away, but he had to call George.

George asked him to meet at the Kahana for dinner at seven. Brad was looking forward to their special grilled mahi-mahi with rice, and pineapple spears.

"Harry only had time to tell me that you had some problems, Brad. Tell me what happened."

"At first, everything was going well.... although I hadn't learned much. Ian contacted me, and told me about one of the crew members actually seeing Chang put a knife in Ingra's back. I don't think he said whether she was pushed or deliberately jumped trying to escape. At that point I didn't know who the man with the Cockney accent was."

"I know. Ian Gillespie is one of our most experienced members. He was with British Intelligence for years after the war. Then he became an International Courier until he retired at sixty. He found that he couldn't stand the quiet life, and tried to free lance. He knew me from his spy days, so he contacted me last year, and is now a regular member of the INS team. He lives in Kailua on the Windward Side."

Brad concluded, "So you and he arranged for the crewman on the *Malaga Badra* to get sick from food served here. Wasn't that taking a chance on your reputation? The Kahana has a fantastic reputation. Or didn't you know?" Brad kidded him.

George laughed. "We didn't tell anyone except him and Captain Tan Wo Lin how the sailor got sick. And I requested the Captain not to advertise that it came from the Kahana. Believe it or not, the Captain appears to be a decent man. But then.... he must be a part of Chang's terrorist ring."

"So that's how Ian was able to get on the crew of the *Malaga*."

"Yes, among other things Ian is an experienced sailor. He was in the British Navy before he entered the spy business."

"All of a sudden I ended up in the cargo hold. What do you think happened? I don't remember talking to anyone about myself, that much. I tried not to make any contradictory statements."

George said, "You could have slipped up on almost anything you said. Sometimes the slightest comment is suspicious. A criminal mind like Chang's is skilled at detecting inconsistencies."

"Ian rescued me from the cargo hold. He probably saved my life. What do you think they would have done to me.... toss me in the drink?"

"One of two possibilities. Chang might have thrown you overboard, tied to an anchor, on the way to Bangkok..... or.... he might have turned you over to ODAM. I'm afraid they would have tortured you to find out about me and the INS."

"Have you learned any more about ODAM, George.... since I talked to you last?"

"Yes. At the last confrontation that Saddam had with the U.S. on the UN inspections.... you remember.... Saddam threatened to shoot down the next U2 reconnaissance flight? I think it was in November of 1997. He was fully backed by the ODAM members who were infuriated by the actions of the United States. Remember that four American businessmen were murdered in Karachi, Pakistan the same week that Saddam was challenging the UN Security Council."

George stopped to nibble on his Sushi before he continued. "Members from the Middle East, and some Asian anti-American groups had a meeting in Bangkok. They met in an area called Pat Pong, known for expensive strip joints and prostitutes. I managed to get one undercover agent, a high price prostitute, in on the meetings. It was the only way. She was a Thai Goddess charging US$2,000 a night. Anyone she chose was considered a VIP. One of the ODAM members took her along to show off.

"She had no political interest in our mission. In fact, she was a cold fish. Her brother is one of our active members, and talked her into it.... for a fee! If you knew what I had to pay her, you'd understand why she helped us. And it was the only possible way to ever have penetrated ODAM. We already have two dead members who tried.... and you know first hand how close it was to three.... if it wasn't for Ian's quick thinking!"

"What did she report to her brother from the meetings?" Brad questioned.

"The ODAM group is paying Chang Hai and Jacque Kamel in Detroit to lead the terrorist strike. She heard one of them say it would be in September on Mackinac Island. She happened to be out of the room whenever the reason was given. She heard them specifically name the Grand Hotel and Mission Point Resort. Something about getting the floor plans. She had to act completely uninterested in their discussions.... so she missed some of the important details."

Brad said, "That agrees with what Jennie told me in Mackinaw City. She was instructed by Jacque to get the floor plans. I haven't talked to her since then."

"When do you go back to Michigan?"

"This is the last weekend for the class.... Friday night and all day Saturday. I planned on leaving on Tuesday. Do you want me to contact this Jennie?" Brad didn't know why he asked. George would tell him in due time.

"You just have a relaxing time.... after your classes.... and then go to the House Without A Key and.... whatever ..... maybe just watch Madelaine dance. That's relaxing.... isn't it?"

"You knew I liked Madelaine.... didn't you George? I really do want to see her. Then I'll head back to Mackinaw City. I have to stop at the Central Michigan University campus in Mt. Pleasant first to turn in my grades."

"Good. In the meantime I'll contact Sam in Detroit to find out what Jennie knows. You'll hear from Sam in a week or so.... or you can call him when you get back to Lansing."

Brad said good-bye to George, and went back to the Royal Hawaiian. Preferring to be completely finished with his class before seeing Madelaine, Brad waited until Monday. He finished grading the quizzes and the term papers. The final grades were not due until he returned to Michigan.

MONDAY, JULY 13

BRAD WALKED OVER TO THE HOUSE WITHOUT A KEY AT SIX-thirty. He selected a quiet spot in the back to have a Mahi-Mahi sandwich and a cup of black coffee with blue sugar. He always drove the waitresses crazy by asking for blue sugar. When they looked puzzled, he would say, "Well there's white sugar, brown sugar, pink sugar, and blue sugar. Saccharin is always pink.... and aspartame is always blue. So I'd like some blue sugar." When they would say, "You mean Equal." He would explain in his pedagogical manner that Equal was the name of only one brand of blue sugar.

At the first intermission Madelaine went directly to Brad's table. "I'm so glad to see you back. How was your trip to.... was it.... Singapore? Did you have a good time?" she politely asked.

"It was wonderful.... I......" He stopped abruptly. Brad couldn't lie to Madelaine.

He displayed a rare outburst of emotion.... with a touch of self-pity. He had kept his fear inside all this time.... never letting it surface. Men are conditioned to do that for the sake of their masculine image. Confronted with a trusting and compassionate woman like Madelaine it finally exploded. His voice was noticeably shaky.

"No.... it wasn't wonderful. I had a terrible time. I was on a foreign ship. And.... I was kidnapped.... then I escaped. It was awful. I was almost killed!"

He knew he shouldn't say anything. But, he trusted Madelaine so much, he had to tell her. He hoped it wasn't just to get her sympathy.... so she would feel sorry for him....

and.... we--ll.... baby him a little! He did lay it on a little thick.

"What are you talking about, Bradley. Are you all right?" Madelaine was worried. He sounded a little confused.... as if he were making it up.

"Yes. I'm perfectly all right now. I had to tell you the truth, even though I shouldn't. It's because I trust you.... and I've grown to like you.... more than a little."

"That makes me happy. Tell me.... now.... what happened on your trip to Singapore? I assumed it was to lecture. Billy and Alina told me that you had lectured before in both Kuala Lumpur and Singapore on the subject of one of your accounting books. So I figured that was why you went there."

"Not this time. I just have to tell you. I'm working for an international group of.... well for the lack of a better word.... it's an anti-crime organization."

"You are?" Madelaine was still uncertain of the veracity of what she was hearing.

"Yes. It is headquartered right here in Honolulu. Now.... this is very important. What I am going to tell you is a matter of life and death.... to all of us. You must never repeat this to anyone else.... even your own sweet mother."

Madelaine giggled. "Don't worry.... she's the last one I would tell. She has a hard time keeping a secret." At this point Madelaine wasn't sure if he was kidding or not.

"The fellow I meet here.... you know.... George...."

"Of course I know George, he's the owner of the Kahana. I have entertained there many times."

"That's not all he is. He's the head of INS, which stands for the Information Network System. That's the name of our group. We are all volunteers to stop crime. It first started here in Hawaii.... and now it's worldwide."

Madelaine listened.... wanting to believe him.... but, still a little ambivalent.

"So on last Tuesday, I boarded a foreign ship, the *Malaga Badra*. I lied to the Captain that I was a reporter on the *Honolulu Star*. I told him that I was looking for another reporter, who was supposed to be on the ship. She was actually murdered. I was supposed to find out why, for George. Anyway.... they let me go on the ship to Singapore, so I could write the story that she was supposed to write. I know this sounds crazy.... but I'm not giving you all the details at once."

Madelaine began to set aside some of her doubt. Brad was too serious and detailed to be joking.

"What girl was murdered? You didn't tell me anything about that."

"I'll start from the beginning. One of George's INS members, a woman named Ingra Jensen, was on the *Malaga Badra*, working for George.... to put it bluntly.... spying for George. The day after the *Malaga* passed by the Mackinac Bridge her body was found on the shore of a lighthouse in the Straits of Mackinac. There are three of us in the area who are members of the INS. Myself, an FBI man, and a local sheriff. We all worked together on the bombing at the Soo Locks two years ago."

Madelaine interrupted, "Wait. I have to dance now. Ben is waving up front. I'll be through in thirty minutes or so."

It gave Brad a chance to order dessert. He asked for Tiramisu, which he had.... and loved.... at Assaggio's Italian Restaurant over in Kailua last year. But the waiter said no and suggested the Pineapple Cheesecake with Macadamia nuts on top. It was good.... with coffee.

This also gave him a chance to enjoy Madelaine's dancing. The last time he was too busy talking to George.

He didn't get a chance to relax and enjoy what millions of tourists pay millions of dollars to see.... the hula dancers, the profile of Diamond Head, the ocean waves splashing on the shore, and the enchanting music, on a warm, moonlit night.

After her stimulating performance, Madelaine sat down at Brad's table, puffing a little.

"Go ahead with your story. I have a half hour before the next show. May I have some of your dessert? It looks so good."

"Here have some.... while I order another piece. What do you want to drink with it?"

"Milk. A glass of milk.... it goes good with cheesecake. Now go on.... go on....!"

"Where was I? Oh yes. When George told me that one of his female agents didn't report in.... and a woman was found dead at the Straits..... it dawned on me, or George, I can't remember who it dawned on first....that there could be a connection. And when George found out that the *Malaga Badra* was at the Straits at about the time the body was found.... well.... that was it."

"Was the body of the woman at the Straits identified as this agent of George's.... this Ingra something?"

"Not really. She was never officially identified. But we know that she is Ingra. That is.... George, Sam, Reino, and I believe that she is definitely Ingra. Sam is the FBI man, and Reino is the County Sheriff. He's also one of my best friends."

Madelaine was having a little difficulty following all of this. "What does it all mean? And why did the people on the ship try to kill you?"

Brad realized that this must be confusing. "I don't know exactly why Chang Hai wanted to kill me."

"Who's Chang Hai?"

Brad apologized. "Sorry Madelaine, I forgot. The Captain of the *Malaga Badra* is Tan Wo Lin and the first mate is Chang Hai. The terrorist group is called ODAM and Chang is one of the leaders. We don't believe that the Captain is a member of ODAM. He just works for the shipping company, which is owned by ODAM. We think that Chang ordered two of his men to kidnap me. They injected me with something, tied me up, and threw me into the hold. I would be dead by now, if it weren't for Ian Gillespie, one of George's men."

"Oh my goodness.... oh my goodness!" Madelaine sounded like one of the little orphan girls in the musical, *Annie*. "Now I understand why you were so shaken by all this."

Brad went on. "I'll have to go back to Mackinac tomorrow.... Tuesday. You know I'd love to stay here longer and.... well.... get to know you better. But this Chang knows who I am now. He may try again to get rid of me. And I'm afraid that anyone I befriend could be in danger too. I don't want you to be involved. I trust you so much that I told you about all this. But, I don't want you to be in danger because of me."

"I'm not afraid. Really. If being with you puts me in danger.... then I love danger."

Brad caught the significance. "Well it still worries me that I might put you there. I'm going back to the hotel now. I'd like to see you before I leave.... but.... "

"Call me when you leave to turn in your rental car and I'll drive you to the airport."

Brad didn't object. He wanted to see her too. The next day she picked him up at the Alamo office nearest the airport. She was dressed in a stunning muu'muu. Around her neck was a beautiful handmade lei. When it was time for Brad to board his United Airlines flight for Chicago, Madelaine could no longer hide her emotions. She walked up to Brad, kissed him gently on both cheeks, and said, "Aloha, Bradley, I will wait for you. Please come back soon."

Out of character, Brad reached out and pulled her toward him, hugging her tightly. Neither said a word. There was more than friendship.... they both knew it.

For Bradley Kendall, the erudite, analytical professor, love had to be unequivocal. He would only love one woman for life. He believed that God wanted him to do things right. And if Madelaine was the right girl, she would too.

His last words were, "Don't worry, Madelaine, I'll be back. And sooner than you might think." Brad knew that he had to see her again.

12.

IT WAS WEDNESDAY MORNING WHEN THE PLANE arrived at the Lansing Airport. Brad was dying for a Cracker Barrel breakfast. He located his Mercedes 300 in the parking lot. It started on the first turn of the key, as usual. This would be the closest he would get to a Cracker Barrel. There were none north of Lansing on Highway 27, but there was one on the west side of Lansing.

He called Sam and asked him to join him there. Sam was anxious to hear from Brad. George had already called him from Honolulu to give him a synopsis of Brad's ominous voyage to Singapore on the *Malaga Badra*.

"I've already had coffee and toast, but I'm still hungry," Sam confessed.

"I'm ordering the works," Brad said. "Two eggs, bacon, sausage gravy on biscuits, and grits."

Sam laughed. "Almost like Bob Evans.... but no fried mush!"

Brad related the entire story of his close call to Sam. He didn't include the personal part about telling Madelaine. He wasn't sure that Sam would approve of his telling her about INS. George might not like it either.... and Sam would surely tell George.

"What's new with Jennie, Sam?"

"I haven't heard from her. I can't contact her.... I don't dare. If Jacque thought for a minute that she had any connection with me, she'd be a dead duck. So I never contact her. I have to wait until she sneaks a message to me."

"Is there anything new with this Jacque guy? Has he done anything suspicious?" Brad wondered.

"No. There's nothing that I consider unusual happening with the ODAM group in Detroit. At least I haven't heard anything more from my sources."

"By the way, have you found out who the Chicago leader is yet?"

Sam said, "No.... and George has never said a word about who it is. Apparently none of the INS members know..... or George would have told me."

"You'd think someone would find out," Brad thought out loud.

"Before you leave, Brad, do you need any back up? I mean.... after the attempt to snuff you out by this Chang Hai character.... do you want protection from the FBI? I can do it officially under the circumstances."

"No. With Reino around, and Wilbert Erbe, the Mackinaw City Police Chief, who is a good friend of mine, too.... I couldn't be safer. On the other hand.... if you have a pretty lady agent in mind.... that's different."

"Nope! The guy I had in mind is nicknamed Gruesome Gus!" Sam's sense of humor was just as creative as Brad's.

"That settles it." At that, a few minutes before noon, Brad took off for Mackinaw City, and Sam went back to his Lansing office. July and August were the heaviest months for traffic going to the northern resort areas in Michigan, but it wasn't too bad on a Wednesday.

It was almost four o'clock when he arrived in Mackinaw City. Brad remembered that he was out of salt rising bread. That was a disaster. He was spoiled rotten. For him, toast just wasn't the same, unless it was salt rising toast. So he drove straight to the Mackinaw Bakery, to make sure they didn't run out. The pleasant young lady at the counter reached for the salt rising bread without being asked.

She then said, "I have one almond croissant left.... would you like it?" She knew he couldn't resist the almond croissants.

"I sure do, Lillian. There's nothing to eat at the cottage. I've been gone for almost three weeks."

The bakery served as one of the town's meeting places. The locals liked to have coffee and doughnuts while they visited with their old friends. In the tourist season it was bustling all day long.

Brad then picked up his mail. In Mackinaw City the post office was another meeting place for the locals. There was no home delivery, so the residents converged there to pick up their mail every weekday morning.

He drove out Lakeside Drive until he passed the cemetery. The cottage was along the Straits less than two miles from town. He had just seen some of the most spectacular scenery in the world.... the Pacific Ocean, the Hawaiian Islands, Asian countries.... but, the natural beauty of the Straits of Mackinac was still exhilarating to him.

No where on earth was there the combination of the longest suspension bridge in the world, the mammoth one-thousand foot ore carriers, the Grand Hotel with its longest porch in the world, the hundreds of foreign freighters from almost every country of registration in the world, and the magical Mackinac Island, with its horse drawn carriages taking us back to the nineteenth century.

Friday, July 24

Brad had spent the past week writing an article for publication in one of the accounting journals. It was always a long shot, but he had to keep trying. One of his articles, the least likely to ever get published.... he thought.... hit the jackpot, and won an award. He was then invited to lecture at the Waldorf Astoria, and asked to write a book on the subject. The book became the basis for his overseas lectures. So you never know.... you have to keep trying.... publish or perish.... you know.

At ten o'clock on Friday night, Jennie knocked on his front door. "Hi there. I'm back."

She said it nonchalantly.... as if her appearance would not be a surprise. It had been hot all day, and it was still light outside. In July it stayed light until slightly after ten o'clock. She had a short-sleeved, low neck, very tight, white T-shirt on, which made her already generous bosom look even more generous. Her T-shirt was tucked into her also tight fitting blue jeans. Brad supposed it was that hippie image she was trying to maintain.

"Come on in, Jennie," Brad said with curiosity. "Would you like something to drink? A Coke.... or 7-Up?"

She grimaced, as if expecting something stronger. "Coke is fine."

"I saw Sam when I flew back from Hawaii. He said that he hadn't heard from you. Is everything all right?"

"Well.... that depends. Jacque wasn't completely pleased with my last trip here. He wants more detail. So I volunteered to come back. I really wanted to see you."

"Oh." That's all Brad could muster until he thought of something neutral to say. "Where are you staying?"

"I'm staying at the Chippewa Hotel on the Island tomorrow night. I didn't get a motel tonight. I.... well I thought that.... you might have an extra bedroom."

"Oh." His computer-like mind was reaching for excuses.... the bed's not made..... there's no food.... the toilet's plugged up. They all sounded too obvious.

He capitulated. "Oh sure. You can sleep in my guest room. It's not fancy.... it's an old bed, and it's not made up."

"I'm not fussy. I'll make the bed. Just show me where the sheets are. But.... I thought you'd want me to sleep in your bedroom."

"Oh sure. My bed is a little nicer. You can sleep there, and I'll sleep in the guest room." Brad was dead serious.

"Forget it! That's not what I meant. I'll sleep here."

When it dawned on Brad what Jennie really meant, he played dumb, to confirm what she probably thought about him anyway.

They made the bed together, and sat down on the front porch, which looked out onto the Straits. The sun had just disappeared over the horizon, as if someone had dropped it into the sparkling waters of Lake Michigan. The sky lit up with bands of orange, pink, and red streaks that were unimaginable to all but the live viewer. For no more than a few minutes the vivid colors danced above the water and streaked high into the sky. Then in a matter of seconds the light from a sun that had already disappeared was dim. The night had made its entrance allowing the full moon to take center stage.

Jennie was rendered speechless, while she absorbed the splendor of a light show that even Disney World couldn't duplicate.

Brad told Jennie what had happened to him while he was overseas.

"You know, Jennie, you had better not be seen with me. If Jacque and Chang Hai get together and connect us you will be in danger. So we can't be seen together here in Mackinac. There could be someone watching either one of us."

Jennie didn't like that. She wanted to be with Brad as much as possible. "Darn it! I don't care. And I'm not worried here in Mackinac. There are none of Jacque's hit men up here."

Brad dropped the subject to please her. After watching a rerun of "Hawaii Five-O" on the Family Channel they watched the eleven o'clock news.

Then Brad said, "I'm ready for bed. You can stay up as long as you want. Here's the remote."

"No. I'm ready for bed too."

Instead of closing her bedroom door, she took her T-shirt off, in full view, revealing a lot more bare skin, but still no more than what you see on any beach in the summer. She then started to take her jeans off, to further tease him.

Brad was embarrassed. "Jennie stop that. My resistance is only so strong.... you know."

"Well.... I was hoping you'd break down and invite me into your bedroom." She gave him a devilish grin. "You can't blame me for trying."

He walked over to her. "Jennie.... I do like you. That's why I don't want you in bed with me. I believe that joining together in true love is a serious commitment, not a one night stand."

"Preacher!" She laughed. "I know you're right. But it's a lot more fun my way. Good night, Bradley. I adore you even if you are a first class party pooper." At that she closed the door with a loud bang!

Brad gave a sigh of relief, and thought to himself. That was a close one. She was pretty tempting. Nice legs....and all that..... aw' forget it and go to sleep.

13.

 The *Malaga Badra* left Singapore on July tenth. It would take less than one day to reach Thailand. Captain Tan Wo Lin was on the bridge with Chang Hai.

The Captain was talking. "How did he manage to escape, Mr. Chang?"

"There had to be a spy on board.... he had to have help. It was the only way he could have escaped. The door of the cargo hold was locked," Chang growled.

Captain Tan added, "And we know who it was.... the Cockney. He left the ship at Singapore and never returned. That is proof enough that he was definitely a spy. It was no coincidence that our regular crewman became ill at the last minute. It was all planned to place the Cockney spy on board to protect the professor. But whom was he spying for?"

Chang Hai said, "For that Hawaii group.... I'm positive. They are the only ones who are clever enough to trace our movements. We must destroy them."

"You know who two of them are now, Mr Chang.... the American professor and the Cockney."

"Yes.... the Cockney is probably an experienced spy.... to be able to engineer such an elaborate escape. He will be difficult to identify.... I am certain. The professor may be easier to identify. He was obviously not an experienced spy. He blundered in here with no protection of his identity. Remember that he gave his own name, we assumed, as a reporter on the *Honolulu Star*. And our sources easily found that no such *Star* reporter existed. That was the work of an amateur."

The Captain said, "That indicates that he probably is indeed, a professor. And if he did use his own name, you will be able to trace him."

When the ship reached port, every member of the crew was anxious to go to Bangkok. It was an exotic city with gold-leaf covered temples everywhere. In the center of the city is an Emerald Buddha, covered with rubies and sapphires. The crew members were more interested in the Pat Pong district, which was well known in the Orient for night life. Some of the crew members spent all of their free time in the strip joints, and sampling the prostitutes.

Chang Hai went to an expensive and elegant night club near the Shangri-La Hotel. It was called the Siam Club. Inside he showed a card to the hostess, who then escorted him to a private room. In the room were five men, members of ODAM. They all stood up to greet Chang Hai. They had the general features of the stereotyped Middle Easterner. They were dressed like they walked right out of the film, *Casablanca*.... white suits, bright colored ties, and Panama hats. The ODAM leader who greeted him had a facial expression that could not hide his arrogant egoism.

"Hello, Mr. Chang. We are anxious to hear of your last voyage."

"Greetings to you, Mr. Sauloo. It was very successful.

Our cargo of furniture was delivered to Detroit and Chicago.

The automatic weapons were not discovered by customs, which indicates that our packing system is well engineered.

This was the second successful voyage this year."

"And not the last." Mr. Sauloo involuntarily sneered whenever he talked. "On your next voyage you must be at the Straits of Mackinac on September twelfth. Your good Captain Tan must leave Bangkok on the appropriate day to allow for any exigencies. He knows that September is the month of hurricanes in the Caribbean. And El Nino has created some irregularities in the weather patterns in the Pacific. We cannot take any chances. Tell him to allow an extra day in both Honolulu and Chicago."

Mr. Sauloo then turned to one of the men, as if he were resuming a conversation that was under way when Chang Hai entered the room. It was the first meeting for this newest member of the group, a sinister looking man named Kochark.

"We in this room represent the major groups that wish to destroy the American infidels. That is why we call ourselves ODAM, the Organization to Destroy AMerica. Their hedonistic customs are being spread throughout the world by their electronic technology. They can now reach our innocent children with their evil movies. They call us ter-rorists.... they are the terrorists. Their teenage children are running wild in their cities, killing and rampaging. They are all on drugs. If you want to join our.... shall we say.... con-sortium.... your sponsors must provide ten million dollars.... in US currency, of course."

He expressed a sinister frown that indicated how repulsed he was with his last statement. "How ironic.... we hate the Americans.... yet, when it comes to money, we trust their currency the most."

"When do you require the money?" The newest member of ODAM asked a logical question.

"It must be deposited in our bank.... you have the infor-mation on where and how in your folder.... by August first. You must also provide one man, your sponsor's most expe-rienced, with automatic weapons and explosives. He must be on the *Malaga Badra* when it leaves Bangkok in August. Mr. Chang Hai is here to provide you with directions and instructions for the voyage. On August first you will be informed of the exact sailing date and time."

Mr. Sauloo hesitated a few seconds before adding, "Are there any other questions?"

The new man asked, "What is the plan? I must know more details to be convinced that this costly strike will be worth the chances that we are taking.... and the ten million dollars."

Mr. Sauloo sneered from habit as he spoke. "A group of congressmen are forming a new ultra-conservative party. Interested members from the two major existing parties will meet on Mackinac Island the weekend beginning

September eleventh. They have invited the Chinese Foreign Minister, Chong Lo Pan, as a guest. He will be the main speaker at the Saturday night banquet. It is a political tactic to embarrass the Democratic President, who has been unable to persuade him to visit the White House. Chong Lo Pan has been unanimously selected by the Chinese leaders to replace the eighty-year-old Zuang Huan Do, who has been seriously ill.

"They intend to make an announcement to the American people that will turn the election around, and insure the new conservative party of victory at the next election. We do not have all of the details of the meetings, yet. Our Detroit member, a man named Jacque Kamel, will obtain the logistical details for us. He is a despicable man, but we must use him."

"What is our motive?" The new member, Kochark, asked. "What do you expect to accomplish by disposing of the Chinese Foreign Minister? Is he that important in international circles?"

Mr. Sauloo answered, "We need to disrupt both governments. They are trying to stop our weapons and drug trade. That is our major source of funds to support our divine mission to rid the world of infidels. The Chinese Foreign Minister, Chong Lo Pan, is too friendly with the Americans. He is beginning to worship the affluence of the western culture, and to believe in free enterprise. Our spies tell us that he has bragged to his supporters that when he replaces Zuang Huan Do, he will stop supplying us with nuclear technology and automatic weapons.

"When we kill him, it will humiliate these conservatives

and cause a permanent rift between China and the Americans. And the elimination of the key conservative leaders will cause chaos in the American government. We will leave evidence that the attack was done by a militia group. The news media will then do the rest. They will put enough doubt in the minds of the people."

Kochark said, "I see.... and it will show them that we can strike wherever we please. The Americans will panic, knowing that they cannot stop us."

Mr. Sauloo then excused Chang Hai, satisfied that all of the arrangements had been made. Chang returned to the *Malaga Badra*. He informed Captain Tan Wo Lin of the plans to leave Bangkok, so that the *Malaga Badra* could arrive at its ominous rendezvous with death, on schedule.

14.

SATURDAY, JULY 25

◆ JENNIE COMPLETED HER MISSION FOR JACQUIE BY obtaining detailed information on Fort Mackinac and the Governor's Summer Residence, which she omitted on her last trip. She spent Saturday night at the Chippewa Hotel. The Chippewa had been recently remodeled with a new dining area and pub. Her room overlooked the harbor between the Marina and the Arnold Lines' Dock. Brad had promised to show her around the Upper Peninsula on Sunday.

Brad met her on Saturday at noon. She wanted to go to lunch at the new tavern and restaurant, called the Depot, in the restored Mackinaw City Railroad Station in the Courtyards. She ordered the crab leg appetizer, while Brad capitulated to his uncontrolled passion for a whitefish sandwich.

"Reino said that's all you ever eat," Jennie commented. Brad did not argue the point.

After lunch they walked to the other side of the Courtyard. They stopped in front of the deli, named Nature's Table. Jennie said, "Let me look at the menu for next time. The veggie chili sure sounds good."

They walked past a Kilwin's Fudge Shop and the movie theatres to the parking lot. Brad drove on Nicolet Avenue to the Bridge entrance near Audie's Restaurant. As they drove across the Mackinac Bridge, Jennie was unusually quiet.

"Does this bother you, Jennie? We are about two hundred feet above the water, you know. Remember when that old man was thrown off the bridge four years ago? It was right about here."

Jennie didn't say a word.

"Yep. He fell the two-hundred feet into the water and kaput.... he was probably squashed to death. And you must remember the car that went over the side. Right over the rail. It was a shock to all of us." Jennie was very quiet.

"And then there was the painter.... he fell sixty.... or was it eighty.... feet into the water, and...."

"Bradley Kendall.... shut! .... up!" Jennie exploded. "One more word and I'll..... I'll push you over the side."

"Gee. I'm sorry Jennie. I didn't know you'd be squeamish." Under his breath he could almost be heard to say, "Women! I'll never understand them."

He drove around to Hessel and Cedarville, at Les Cheneaux Islands. The marinas were busy with pleasure boats and fishing charters. Jennie stopped at the quaint Safe Harbor Bookstore to buy a gift for her niece.

He drove northward to Pickford, which was not far from Rudyard. Brad always wondered if they were named for

Mary Pickford and Rudyard Kipling, but no one ever seemed to know. He drove to Barbeau so Jennie could see the Rock Cut, the narrow down bound passage for the freighters.

Brad drove along, as close as he could get, to the St. Mary's River toward Sault Ste. Marie. He was on the way to the Soo Locks, where the ships and products from all over the world converge on one narrow point, and are slowly lifted up twenty-two feet into the largest, deepest and most fascinating fresh water lake on the planet, Lake Superior.

Brad drove into Sault Ste. Marie and parked in front of the popular Lockview Restaurant directly across from the Visitor's Center. Inside he showed Jennie the models of the four Locks, the MacArthur, the Sabin, the Davis, and the Poe.

Brad explained to Jennie, as if he were a tour guide, "The Poe Lock is not only the largest lock in the world.... it is the only lock in the entire St. Lawrence Seaway System wide enough to hold the fourteen 105-foot wide lakers. There are only thirteen 1,000 footers, but the 858-foot *Roger Blough*, named after a former president of the United States Steel Company, is 105-feet wide."

"How do you know all this stuff, Brad?" She was thrilled. It was her first time at the Soo Locks.

"My dad used to write articles about the ships and the Straits for the *Mackinaw Marquee*, the free tourist paper in Mackinaw City. I grew up with it."

They climbed up to the Visitor's Tower just in time to see the *Ziemia Gnieznienska*, a 591-foot salty from Poland enter the MacArthur Lock.

"How do you pronounce that one?" Jennie yelped excitedly.

"Well the first name is pronounced just the way it looks.... zeem-me-ah.... but, I don't know how to pronounce that giz-nin-ska business. There's hundreds of foreign salties that enter the Seaway system every season."

"What's a salty?"

"Salty refers to the fact that it's an ocean going freighter.... a salt water ship."

"You said the Poe Lock was the largest in the world. I always thought the Panama Canal and the Suez Canal had the biggest locks in the world," Jennie confessed.

"Well, the locks in the Panama Canal are large enough to handle battleships and ocean cruisers. They are all 1,000-feet long and 110-feet wide, but the Poe Lock is a little longer, 1,200-feet long by 110-feet wide, making it the biggest. The Suez Canal doesn't have any locks at all."

"Don't the lake freighters go on the ocean?"

"They could. All the Canadian freighters are built to go through the entire Seaway System. Only the 1,000-footers and the *Roger Blough* are locked in."

"Why?" She sounded like Brad's five-year-old niece who always said why to everything. One day, in response to her repeated whys, Brad said, "Why do you think?" She stopped to think, and came up with the obvious answer. From then on Brad knew how to answer her whys.

"The reason is the width, not the length. All locks in the St. Lawrence Seaway system are eighty feet wide. The 1,000-footers are 105-feet wide. But, more than that the lakers are not designed for the ocean waves."

"Why?" Jennie did it again.

"Why do you think?" Brad tried his successful system on her.

"I have no idea. Why would I ask you if I knew?"

Oh! Oh! He found out that his system didn't work on an adult. "Sorry, Jennie. The ocean waves are farther apart and.... it's a long story. It's mainly a design difference in the shape and length of the ships. The *Middletown*, a laker built in 1943 was the only laker known to have shot down an enemy plane in World War II. So some lakers were used for the war effort on the ocean. There were no 1,000-footers back then, anyway. The *Middletown*, which was renamed the *USS Neshanic* during the war, was only 730-feet long."

Even some tourists surrounding them on the crowded Visitor's Tower were listening to his encyclopedic barrage of information.

A little boy piped up, thinking Brad was a guide. "Mister, how long is that boat in the big tub down there?"

Brad said with authority, "I don't have my book with me.... but I would say that it is about 600-feet long."

Brad knew that most salties were in the 550 to 600 foot range, with a few below 500 feet, and very few up to 700 feet. His visual estimate told him that this ship was slightly under 600-feet long.

A listening tourist, who was holding his small daughter up to see the ship chimed in, "Hey kid.... the lady inside said it was 591-feet long. She wrote it on that chalk board behind the counter."

"Thank you mister.... and you too.... mister," The boy politely said after a nudge from his mother.

Brad decided he'd better keep quiet. And Jennie was getting to the ho hum stage with Brad's academic prowess. Jennie and Brad were both hungry. They went across the street and walked into the Lockview Restaurant, Brad stopping to fill the parking meter first. Even Jennie noticed the curious wooden ship models on the tables, and on the beams overhead. She opted to go up to the second floor dining room in order to see the Locks better.

A cute, young Scandinavian-looking blonde waitress said, "Hello, Professor Kendall. You prob-ly don't remember me. I had you in ACC 220, the required Management Accounting course up at LSSU. I won't forgit.... I got my first C."

Brad was used to hearing the moans and groans about the first C.... from the students who had never had a real challenge, until they took their first accounting course.

The waitress added, "Too bad you missed the Friday Night Special, all the fish you can eat.... perch and white-fish."

Jennie was getting uneasy with this pretty waitress standing over them. "Let's order. I'll have the fried shrimp dinner."

Brad had already tried to talk her into the perch, but she preferred the shrimp. "I'll have the perch in a basket," he decided instead of his usual whitefish sandwich.

After dinner they headed back to the Straits and to Mackinaw City. Jennie asked to stay overnight again.

"I didn't make a reservation for tonight here in Mackinaw City. And I didn't want to stay overnight on the Island again.... after spending all day traveling and going to the Sault with you. I was going to make a reservation after we got back.... but you saw the motel signs.... Sorry!.... Sorry!..... No Vacancy! What more could I do?"

Brad was faking an expression of artificial resistance, deliberately trying to tease her.

Jennie pleaded, "I promise to behave. I'll close my door when I undress.... and I won't sneak into your room in the middle of the night..... even though the women on television do it all the time! I'll even make coffee for you in the morning.... and maybe salt rising toast."

Brad finally capitulated. "Throw in two eggs and bacon, and I'll let you stay."

"All right! I'll do it.... thank you.... Brad." She said it with glee as she threw her arms around his neck and hugged him tight. She was uninhibited. During her hippie days, the girls hopped into bed with any man who was willing.... and there was no scarcity of those. She was programmed to thrust her female engines into full gear, whenever a desirable man turned the key. Brad didn't deliberately turn the key.... he just accidentally opened the door to her enthusiasm.

Brad felt that scrumptious, soft, curvaceous feminine body of hers squirm into all the crevices of his masculine susceptibility. He gracefully pushed her away.... but not until he enjoyed the illusion of the potential outcome of the joining of God's two favorite creations..... the male and the female.

That night Jennie was a good girl after Brad tactfully expressed his convictions about how important it was to him to follow his Christian beliefs about moral and ethical behavior. The serious moment brought up the situation she was in.

"I am in a terrible spot, Brad. Jacque still trusts me, or he wouldn't send me here. At one time I wanted to help him.... but now that I know how treacherous he is, I don't want to be any part of it."

"I understand, Jennie. Now you just can't walk away from it. Jacque wouldn't let you. When we get to the end of this.... whatever it is.... their big surprise in September, Sam can give you protection."

"A lot of good that will do. I'd have to go in hiding for life."

"How about changing your name and identity? And moving out of Dearborn, naturally."

"Sounds easy.... but all my friends are there.... and I spent most of my life around Detroit."

"Maybe Sam, or the local police, or whoever has juris-diction.... can put Jacque in jail for life."

"I hope so. He has a hit man.... you know. Everyone calls him Garlic. I know.... it sounds weird... it's 'cause he smells like garlic. He has straight dark hair, and a little bald-ing on the top of his forehead. He's about average height, and has a short, pointed beard. Looks dangerous.... and he is."

"How does he treat you?"

"He comes on to me when Jacque isn't around. Squeezes me in the wrong places.... then I slap him. But he never goes any farther. So I don't tell Jacque. Garlic might not like it."

"Good idea. You don't want to double cross a guy like that. What do you say we go to bed?"

"Great idea.... which bedroom shall we go in?"

Before Brad's face could indicate his response, she said, "Just kidding! I had my bible sermon already tonight, so I know the proper way to behave. You go in your bed.... and I go in mine. Good night....!"

Then she whispered to herself, "Mister goody-goody two shoes."

15.

◆ JENNIE DROVE HOME THE NEXT DAY, AND BRAD resumed work on his accounting articles at the cottage. On the following Wednesday Jennie reported to Jacque on her visit to Mackinac Island.

"Good work, Jenn! I think they should be satisfied with this."

"Who should be satisfied?" she asked, knowing that he would be evasive.

"You don't have to know, honey. You just let me do the thinkin'. It's better you don't know who I work for. One slip-up and they wouldn't hesitate for a minute to snuff us out."

"They couldn't touch you with Garlic around.... could they?"

"These guys are international kingpins. They're behind the big terrorist attacks. Remember the four American businessmen in Pakistan.... and the sixty tourists gunned down in Egypt? This group coordinates the terrorist strikes all over the world. Garlic would be mincemeat compared to these guys."

Jennie was amused at Jacque's unintended simile. "Why would you want to get involved with such dangerous creatures?"

"What do you think? Big moolah! Half a million dollars if we do exactly as they say. I just have to make sure their Detroit boys get their automatic weapons and...."

"And.... what?" Jennie explored.

"None a your business, Jenn."

"I know. It's some kind of explosive I'll bet," she pushed.

"I don't really know, Jenn, except that it's something new.... and deadly."

O

GOVERNOR DAN BROADWELL RECEIVED A CALL FROM WASHING-ton, DC. It was Nate Goodrich, the junior Senator from Michigan. Nate was a native of Grand Rapids.

"Dan. This is Nate. I have most of the arrangements made. There will be between forty and fifty members attending. It isn't too hard to convince them to go to Mackinac Island. It will start on Friday, September eleventh through Sunday. Some of them want to come early with their families. I told them they can make those reservations themselves with the Grand Hotel or the Mission Point Resort."

"Good work, Nate. You and your wife will stay at the Governor's Mansion with me and Eugenia. The Chinese Foreign Minister.... umm!.... what's his name?"

"Chong Lo Pan, Dan."

"Oh yea.... anyway.... this Chong Lo Pan should stay at the Grand. He should enjoy the pomp and circumstance.... and the elegance of the Grand Hotel."

Nate added, "He'll bring a retinue of people with him. I don't know who they all are yet.... but, I will get clearance for them all from the Foreign Office."

○

IT WAS JUST BEFORE MIDNIGHT ON SATURDAY, AUGUST FIRST. THE sky was darkened with hazy clouds. The 1996 four-door Oldsmobile 98, with a sleepy young woman at the wheel, pulled into the roadside park north of Flint, Michigan. There were no cars in the parking lot. While she was in the women's rest room, a black, two-door Toyota Camry pulled in front of the service building and parked. A man with straight dark hair and a short, pointed beard walked to the building and stood behind some bushes next to the walkway.

Five minutes later she walked outside and breathed in the comfortably cool summer air. Just as she noticed that there were now two cars in the parking lot, a powerful arm reached out and pulled her into the bushes. She could see the silencer of a pistol pointing at her head, just as the muffled blast ended her earthly dreams. It was a pity that her very last sense of smell on earth was that of garlic.

○

BRAD HAD BEEN BUSY WORKING ON HIS CURRENT JOURNAL ARTIcle after Jennie left Mackinac. He finally turned the television on for the Monday night news. The six o'clock news was on with Dave and Pallas of Channel 7 & 4. Dave was announcing:

> The body of a young woman was found at a roadside park north of Flint, Michigan. The name of the victim will be withheld until the family has been notified. There were no witnesses. The woman was shot two times in the head at close range. Local and state police say that they have no clues as to who might have murdered the woman.

○

TWO DAYS LATER PROFESSOR BRADLEY KENDALL RECEIVED A CALL from Sam Green in Detroit. "Did you hear the news about a woman murdered at a roadside park up near Flint?"

"Yes. They didn't say much about it.... why?"

"It was Jennie Burke."

Brad was shocked. "Oh my God.... No Sam.... No! It can't be.... It's my fault." Tears came to his eyes.

Sam was surprised by the degree of Brad's response. "What do you mean it was your fault?"

"She came up here last week. Jacque sent her to get more information on the Island. I didn't want her to be seen with me.... but she insisted. After she finished her job for Jacque, we took a drive up to the Sault, and around the area. She wanted to see everything.... you know.... how the city people love the UP. I warned her that someone may have identified me after that Singapore thing."

"I don't think that's the reason she was killed, Brad."

"What.... really? What do you mean?"

"Remember the friend.... Joyce?"

"Sure. She was a nice girl. We had a lot of fun. I think she liked Reino."

Sam went on, "Well.... she came to see me yesterday. It seems that Jennie told her quite a bit about Jacque, and even about her cooperating with me. They were roommates. They lived in the same apartment in Dearborn, you know."

"No I didn't know that. I just knew they were friends."

"Joyce said that Jacque went through her purse and found the bill from the Chippewa Hotel.... for one night only. He knew she was gone for three nights. And she had already lied to him that she stayed at the Chippewa for all three nights. By the way. Did she stay at your place?"

Brad was embarrassed. "She.... kind of talked me into it. But no monkey business. I made her stay on her own side."

"Of the bed?"

"No.... of the cottage. You know I have two bedrooms. And you know how I feel about pushy women. But.... it was late, and she needed a room. The motels are full on the weekends in the busy season. She tried to.... you know.... but, I made her behave. I feel terrible talking about her this way. She was a sweet girl.... I liked her a lot. She couldn't help it if she was in that.... generation of weirdos."

Sam said, "She didn't have to join up with that Jacque Kamel guy. We'd love to pin a rap on him. We know he's ordered quite a few killings.... but, we can't nail him down. His boy, Garlic, does the dirty work."

"Garlic.... are you kidding?" Brad chuckled.

"No, that's what they call him. This guy's real name is Gar Locke. So.... what do you think all the kids called him back when he was in grade school?"

"Then you and I know who killed Jennie," Brad said.

"Sure. But, we have absolutely no evidence.... except.... one of the emergency workers first at the scene said he thought he smelled garlic on her body. Imagine how that would stand up in court, with no other evidence. I had the locals check Garlic out. But, he was clean. They couldn't tie him to the scene or the gun. He had witnesses who claimed he was in Detroit that night."

"What else did Joyce say.... anything helpful?"

"Oh yea. I was going to say that Joyce told me Jennie really spewed it out to her for the first time. Before this she had never talked about Jacque to Joyce. She said that Jennie explained to Jacque that she stayed in one of the small motels outside of town for a couple of nights because the big ones were all full. He wondered why she stayed so long in Mackinaw City. She explained that she loved Mackinaw, and the Island, and just wanted to enjoy it longer. She said that Jacque acted suspicious when she left."

"I suppose there's no way to pin anything on Jacque.... just like Al Capone. Tax evasion is your only hope." Brad recalled the Capone stories.

"Yes.... except we're getting a lot more squealers now from the inside. That is.... if they aren't rubbed out like Jennie. She heard plenty while she was with Jacque. But, I don't know if she actually saw enough to put him away. Jacque was too careful for that."

"Thank you for calling me, Sam. It was terrible news about Jennie.... but, I appreciate your letting me know. I might have found out from the television.... and that would have been a worse shock."

16.

◆ CAPTAIN TAN WO LIN HAD CALCULATED THE EXACT date of departure in order to assure the arrival of the *Malaga Badra* at the Mackinac Bridge on September eleventh. On Friday August seventh, the five terrorists provided by the ODAM leaders had boarded the ship at Bangkok, three days before the ship was scheduled to leave. Each terrorist had to be familiar with the ship in order to serve as a crew member.

They were the most cold-blooded, vicious terrorists that could be found by each ODAM leader, but they had not all served on an ocean going ship. The regular crew was reduced to a minimum. The terrorists would only have to act as crew members when the ship entered the St. Lawrence Seaway System, where either a Canadian or an American pilot was required to be on board.

Six days later the *Malaga Badra* reached Honolulu from

Singapore. Chang Hai was talking to Captain Tan. "I will be leaving you now my dear Captain. I have an appointment with the American professor."

"Did you find out who he is, Mr. Chang?"

"Yes. He made the mistake of using his real name.... which proves that he is an amateur. Our ODAM computer system identified him as a professor of Accounting at Lake Superior State University at.... how do you say.... Salt Saint Mah-ry? He was somehow connected with that woman who.... disappeared from our ship."

"We know that he was not, in fact, a reporter on the *Honolulu Star*, as he claimed.... do we not?" Captain Tan asked rhetorically.

"That was most certainly a lie. My conclusion is that he is a spy for the Honolulu group. He therefore must be eliminated. And that is why I am leaving the ship. I do not intend to say more. You are not to be a party to the.... shall we say.... more severe activities of our benefactors. They pay me well for what I do and they pay you well to operate this ship.... and to remain apart from any suspicious activities. They have given me specific orders to that effect."

"And I am well pleased to remain apart from.... shall we say.... the more severe activities.... as you so delicately describe them, my dear Mr. Chang."

Chang Hai then departed from the *Malaga Badra* and walked to downtown Honolulu. After spending days on a ship most of the crew members enjoyed the mere act of walking on land. Downtown Honolulu was not far from the Honolulu Harbor and provided a delightful walk in the always pleasant Hawaiian climate.

Honolulu does have an assortment of the usual pleasure attractions for the crews of the foreign ships that dock at the harbor, and for the soldiers and sailors at the US military bases. What is surprising is that the Hawaiian Islands do not have an abundance of the lascivious entertainment attractions. It is a family tourist attraction, and is relatively free from drugs and major crime.

It must have taken a great deal of imagination to conjure up all those crime scenes depicted on "Hawaii Five-O". Even Wo Fat was sheer make-believe, named after a restaurant. For most of the *Malaga Badra's* crewmen, just being in Honolulu, Waikiki, Pearl City, Hawaii Kai, and the surrounding towns was a treat.

○

LATER THAT AFTERNOON A PASSENGER NAMED KAM LEE, WHO looked surprisingly like Peter Lorre, boarded the United Airlines flight to Chicago with a connection to the Lansing Airport arriving early Monday morning on August seventeenth.

He rented a car at the airport, where he received a free map of Michigan, and directions to the nearest shopping center. He was looking for a Chinese restaurant. He found one named the Mandarin Gardens and ordered his favorite, Moo Goo Gai Pan.

When he located Sault Ste. Marie on the map, a flurry of words came out, unrecognizable to any English speaking customers. The expression of embarrassment on the petite Chinese waitress's face indicated the irreverent nature of the flurry. The distance was enormous to one who was used to driving in Singapore or Hawaii. Over there he might not drive the equivalent distance to Sault Ste. Marie and back, almost six hundred miles, in a week.... or maybe a month.

Chang Hai, or shall we say, Kam Lee, the current alias he was using for this self-appointed assignment, changed his identity frequently when he traveled. George and the INS system kept track of all the major international criminals, spies, and terrorists. Sharp operators like Chang soon realized that they were being tracked, and made adjustments to outsmart the system. Chang Hai didn't know who was responsible, but he knew they operated out of Hawaii. That was because in the early days the INS only tracked drug dealers entering Hawaii.... and Chang was one who had been intercepted by an INS squad. They didn't have authority to arrest suspected drug dealers, but they could block their entry into Hawaii.

Chang drove as far as Gaylord the first day. It was a long drive for him. He stayed at a Comfort Inn, asking for a good restaurant.

"Do you want a Chinese restaurant?" The clerk asked.

"No.... please.... American food will be all right." Chang was ready to try something different.

"The Sugar Bowl is very good.... and there's the new Brewery. It's popular too. There's lot'sa good restaurants here in Gaylord."

Chang was satisfied with chicken noodle soup and tea at the Sugar Bowl. He then settled down for the night, studying the map once more. The next morning he was on his way to Mackinaw City. The road construction on Interstate 75 was something new to him. He was happy when the traffic slowed down. He was not used to driving on the wrong side of the road. Most of his driving was in Singapore and Hong Kong.

When he reached Mackinaw City the village was crowded with tourists. Every parking space on the main street was taken. After all it was August eighteenth, the peak of the season. The new Courtyard shops were bustling with curious tourists, while the nostalgic shops on main street were busy keeping up with the happy-go-lucky families from all over the world.

Chang drove along Huron Street, viewing the spectacular Mackinac Bridge for the first time. He turned by Audie's Restaurant onto the Bridge. He drove slower as he neared the center of the enormous Bridge, to enjoy the view of the Straits from above. It reminded him of the Strait of Malacca between Malaysia and Indonesia.

He stopped for gas at the Shell station on the St. Ignace side of the Bridge, asking directions to make sure he was on the right track. His pronunciation of the regional names were barely understandable, but the local merchants were used to that. Chang spoke many languages.... but not French.

"The sign on this road points that way to Man-is'-ta-cue and Es-can'-a-bah. That is wrong way to Salt-Saint-Mah'-ry....no?"

"You wanna go to the Soo? Just take a left past the Bridge, an' yer on the way, mister. Fifty miles an' git off at exit three ninety-two. You'll practically drive straight into a Walmart, Penney's, and the works. You prob-ly want the casinos.... well, there's one to your left before you get to the

Soo.... it's at a little town called Brimley. But that's a few miles out. The big one is in the Soo....when you get halfway downtown.... you just turn right and keep drivin'.... you can't miss it!"

Chang had heard that one many times before, from Englishmen. "You caw'nt miss it" seemed to be their favorite direction.

Chang said thanks and followed his directions to the Soo. He had no intention of going to a casino. That is for the stupid Occidentals, he mused. They are always looking for something for nothing. They are too lazy to work.

Less than an hour later he was pulling off the thruway into the edge of Sault Ste. Marie. He registered as Kam Lee at a new Hampton Inn. He had already obtained the address of a Professor Bradley Kendall.

Brad had rented Reino's house on Riverside Drive right on the St. Mary's River. He felt at home there because he could see the freighters pass by along the narrow section of the river, and he had spent many an hour visiting Reino when he lived there.

At three o'clock on Wednesday morning Chang quietly left the motel. He drove straight down Ashmun Street to downtown. He was told to turn right at Portage Street and drive along until, about two miles out of town, it became Riverside Drive. He reached the address, noticing that there was no car in the driveway. It could be in the garage, of course. The garage was old and dilapidated. It looked too small for a big car. Chang just gave a humph sound. He couldn't explain everything he encountered in life.... he thought to himself.

He parked along the street. He then began to adroitly pry open the seventy-year-old lock on the back door of the house. He surreptitiously walked into the bedroom. He had a knife in his hand, ready for use, until it was clear that no one was in the house. Chang never carried a gun. His knife was the only weapon he used. This knife was special.... it had belonged to his father. Chang had used it many times in his line of work. Although he was not a large man, he could kill with his bare hands, when necessary.

He looked at the papers on Brad's desk until he found the address of the cottage in Mackinaw City. He was self-critical at the thought that he was so careless in not assuring that the professor would be home. But in this business.... and being in a completely foreign culture.... these Americans have strange, and unfamiliar, customs.... he rationalized that he was excused for his failure. He would correct his mistakes tomorrow.... or as soon as he ascertained the whereabouts of the elusive professor.

The mental turmoil of failure and disappointment kept him wide awake. A huge sign at the corner ahead, with the smiling face of Kenny Rogers, pointed left to the Kewadin Casino. He turned, thinking that he might as well see this big casino. He couldn't sleep now anyway. He followed the signs for a mile or so. Then he spotted the huge buildings.... huge for that area.... and drove into the parking lot.

People were hovering around the tables, and standing at the slot machines, robotically pulling the handles, even in the middle of the night. Crazy people.... he thought to himself. He bought a roll of nickels, and proceeded to drop them, one by one, into a one-armed bandit. Then the bell rang ..... nickels poured out..... even Chang was excited. But, ten minutes later, the winnings went right back into the machine, until they were all gone. He tried another roll. Gobble.... gobble.... gobble.... the nickels poured into the one-armed monster, whose appetite was endless. He had spent four American dollars.

"Enough, I am throwing money away. What a fool I am!" He mumbled to himself.

He drove back to the motel and retired for the night. The next morning he asked the clerk where to eat breakfast. She said that Studebaker's was very good and was close by. Chang Hai found the restaurant easily and ordered an American breakfast.... two eggs, fried over easy.... whatever that meant.... and two pancakes, two sausages, and.... coffee? "No... No... No! No coffee.... a cup of Oolong tea!

You have no Oolong tea? Any tea .... any tea will do.... but no coffee."

After breakfast Chang headed for Mackinaw City to find the evasive professor. He drove over the Mackinac Bridge, once again amazed by its grandeur. He checked in at a Travelodge Motel. He fell asleep until late afternoon. He was hungry again, but he had enough of that *Amelican* food.

He discovered Chee Peng on Nicolet Street and devoured the tangiest Vietnamese dish.

"I am a visiting professor at the University of Michigan," he told the pretty, Asian-looking waitress. "I am looking for Professor Bradley Kendall. He and I are conducting a research project together. Do you know how I might find him?"

The waitress said, "I know who he is. He comes in here to eat. You drive to the light at the corner.... at the IGA grocery store.... and turn left. Go past the cemetery and turn at Cedar Street. Drive straight for a short block and turn left along Wenniway. Then look for the sign with his name on it."

"How far down that street is it?"

"Only a few houses down."

Chang finished his dinner off with his precious Chinese tea and opened his fortune cookie. It read, "You will soon meet with the opportunity of a lifetime. Do not pass it up, and you will be rich!" The pragmatist Chang Hai did not believe in fortunes or chance. He depended on his own prowess for his good fortune. This time he would not hurry. He would wait for the opportune time to strike.

The next day, he drove around the town. He drove from the Shepler Ferry Line's elaborate entrance on North Huron Road, along the lake front, to the Fort. He turned and drove down Lakeside Drive to Wenniway. He drove slowly past Brad's cottage. A car was in the drive, assumed by Chang to be the professor's. He decided to observe for a day or two before striking. He didn't want to make a mistake again.

17.

◆ Brad hopped in his 1990 Mercedes 300 and drove the almost two miles into town. Mackinaw City was bustling as he tried to find a parking space at the post office. Some locals were upset with the tourists who filled the fifteen minute parking spots in front of the post office. All local residents had to pick up their mail. It wasn't delivered to the door in villages as small as Mackinaw City. It didn't look too small in the summer, with ten thousand visitors in town, but the government won't count the tourists as permanent guests.

He waited until he saw the white back up lights of a car pulling out from a spot in front of the post office and snatched the spot without hesitation. He picked up his mail, stopping to chat with some of his local friends. After throwing out the fifty percent junk mail and advertisements.... he perused the bills and took off for Arnold Ferry

Lines. He parked the Mercedes and walked to the dock, where long lines of tourists were waiting for the one-thirty Catamaran to Mackinac Island.

The Island Express was filled to capacity with tourists bustling with enthusiasm. As the large Cat reached the center of the Straits a red-hulled foreign freighter was passing under the Bridge. Brad could have told the tourists around him that it was a *Federal* something or other, but he didn't want to sound like a smart aleck. He recalled the time with Jennie at the Soo Locks when he ended up as a tour guide for the people on the Visitor's Tower.

He knew it was a leased or chartered ship owned by Fednav Marine of Montreal. They are almost all salties with a red hull. Fifteen or twenty of their ships start with the name *Federal*. As they approached Mackinac Island the ferry and the salty came closer together. Sure enough it was the *Federal Polaris*, registered in Japan.

The *Federal Fuji* is registered in Liberia, operated by a Japanese company, and owned by Fednav of Canada. Isn't that interesting? He would gladly have told all the tourists around him this wonderful information.... but.... no one asked. And he wasn't about to just blurt it out. He usually waited until some kid shouted, "Look at that big boat, Mommy. What is it?"

From that moment on the tourists would have received a barrage of information about the 1,000 footers.... the salties..... the routes, and anything and everything. Kids had a million questions. And this boring accounting professor who shouldn't know a thing about anything, but debits and credits, had a million answers. But, since no one asked any questions.... Brad didn't say a word.

When the Island Express docked, the tourists jumped up and waited in line. Then they poured off the Cat as if it were on fire. Brad just sat until the crowd thinned, and then walked right off. It was always a pleasure to step off the ferry boat onto Mackinac Island. It was the same feeling he had when the plane landed in Hawaii. A place apart from reality. A haven from the real.... sometimes severe.... world.

The Belgians, Percherons, and the Clydesdales put you into this make believe world instantly. Cars were a thing of the past. Stress and worry were anachronistic concepts, not yet discovered here in this Shangri-La.

You wouldn't dare talk about Kennedy, or Elvis, or the Beatles. People would think you're crazy. It was the nineteenth century here.... it had to be .... look around you. Horse drawn drays and bicycles delivered the merchandise and food to the stores and hotels. The automobile hadn't been invented yet on this Island of Paradise.

Brad snapped out of his dream when he saw a man pull out a cellular phone and start talking. Some tourists would never leave their real world behind. Brad had an appointment with Governor Broadwell, who was spending the weekend at the Governor's Summer Residence. He walked to the Chippewa and turned left along Fort Street. It was a steep climb up, past Fort Mackinac to the top of the hill. He stopped to enjoy the view. It was a good place to see the harbor, and the narrow passageway between Mackinac Island and Round Island.

He walked down Huron Road a short distance to the Governor's Mansion, a beautiful old structure built in 1901. It was purchased by the State of Michigan in 1945, when it became officially called the Governor's Summer Residence.

Reino answered the door. "What are you doing here, Reino?"

"Hi Brad. The Governor called me, too. I don't know what it's all about either."

Governor Broadwell was a likeable fellow.... and a real politician. He seemed to be a sincere and honest Governor, to Brad and Reino both.

"Gentlemen. I'm sure that you two are anxious to know why I summoned you so secretly. You must have noticed Brad, that Reino answered the door. No one else is here with us. I shooed the housekeeper and my chauffeur out to town. I knew they were dying to go over to Mackinaw. They both love to go to Anna's Country Buffet."

Brad said, "Well.... I'm certainly honored.... no matter what the reason is.... to be here."

"Me too.... me too!" Reino quickly chimed in.

"The reason is that your friend George from Hawaii asked me to meet with you. He said you two, and Sam Green, would tell me what's going on that might be of interest to the Governor. Sam was on a drug bust somewhere in Wayne County. I couldn't get in touch with him just yet. Now, what in heaven's name did George mean?"

"Did he give you a general idea what it's about?"

"No. He just said that he couldn't talk about it over the phone, and that you two, and Sam, must meet with me privately."

"It's a long story, Governor. I'll start and Reino can fill in what I forget to mention. First, the woman who was found at the foot of the Round Island Lighthouse. She was one of George's INS agents.... or members.... we are called. You know about the INS, of course?"

"Yes. I have cooperated with George on several occasions."

Brad continued, "Well.... this Ingra Jensen.... was murdered when she was on the *Malaga Badra*, a foreign ship registered in Bangkok. We know that it was passing through the Straits the night before the body was found."

"Wait! Wait! Why don't the state police.... and your Governor know this? It's my state.... for goodness sakes."

"You know the rules, Governor. The INS is given the authority to keep silent while they investigate, or if a threat to your state's security is involved. That's exactly why he called you now. He wants you to know.... even if the state police don't know the facts. Reino here is a member of INS.

"Otherwise, even as the investigating Sheriff, he wouldn't know yet who the murdered girl was."

Reino added, "Sam Green is an INS member, too. Otherwise the FBI wouldn't know either."

The Governor asked, "How many members of INS are there in Michigan?"

"We're the only three members in Michigan. The only reason that Brad is a member is because he worked with us on the Soo Locks bombing."

Brad said, "I went to Hawaii and boarded the *Malaga Badra* hoping to find out why Ingra Jensen was killed. It's a long story, but I'll summarize. I was kidnapped and almost killed. I was rescued by one of George's men and returned safely to Honolulu and finally here."

"Go on.... go on." The Governor listened.

"George has discovered that the ODAM group.... you know about them.... don't you?"

"Yes. George keeps me informed of the Detroit branch of ODAM."

Brad continued, "We have reason to believe that the ODAM group is planning to strike in Michigan. They are going to threaten the new Conservative Party's strategy meetings in September."

"That is terribly serious." The Governor's interest was elevated at that statement. "What should I be doing.... and how will I know what is happening?"

"From now on you will know everything that Reino and I know. There's no problem when you're here in Mackinac, but, when you're in Lansing, we'll need instant phone access to you at the Governor's Office. Would you please give it to Reino?"

Brad went on, "That's the point of this meeting, Governor. George wants you to know about the threat.... but, we all must wait for the right moment. He has a chance to expose them.... and to eliminate them, once and for all. Sam will have his FBI anti-terrorist team ready. We think we know where, and approximately when, they plan to strike. If they suspect that we know, they would merely change their plans. If they did.... George would have to start all over again!"

The Governor was a reasonable man. "I will cooperate with you fully. But, I can't jeopardize the safety of the people of the State of Michigan." He sounded just a little like a politician there.... but, he was right.

"No, you can't..... and you still might want to cancel the meetings," Brad said.

"From what you have told me, George would prefer that I do not cancel the meetings. You know about the Chinese Foreign Minister coming to meet with us, I presume."

Brad said, "Yes.... I can't remember his name though."

The Governor said, "It's Chong Lo Pan. Could he be the reason for the threatened attack?"

"George is not sure. It could be that he and the politicians..... sorry..... congressmen are the targets. You recall the young woman who was murdered at the roadside park about three weeks ago?"

"I certainly do. Sam called me right away to tell me that he had the situation under control, regardless what the TV and newspapers said. He told me then that he would be contacting me later about another important matter. I know now that this must have been the other matter."

Brad continued, "Her name was Jennie. She was feeding Sam, and recently me and Reino, information on the activities of the Detroit ODAM group. She was instructed by the leader, Jacque Kamel, to obtain the floor plans of both the Grand Hotel and Mission Point Resort. I believe she was also told to describe the Governor's Mansion.... I mean Residence.... to Jacque. So that is why we suspect that Mackinac Island is the target."

Reino added, "It's also a possibility that they deliberately let us think it is. It seems strange that we have so many indications that this area is the target."

"I never thought of that, Reino." Brad was impressed by Reino's analytical prowess.

"It makes sense," Governor Broadwell agreed. "What better way to be successful than to create a diversion. They may very well be planning to bomb the Capitol Building or a big city."

Brad added, "I'm sure that both George and Sam have considered all possibilities. George has studied the actions of ODAM and has unbelievable sources."

Then Governor Broadwell had that serious look of revealing a secret on his face. "Do you remember what happened here at the Governor's Residence a few years ago, when I was Lieutenant Governor? Governor Hansler was killed along with some former Nazi conspirators."

"My professor and good friend, Roy Nelson, told me all about it," Brad said.

Governor Broadwell continued, "Everyone assumed that Hilda, who was thought to be Hitler's daughter, was killed in the shootout. I have discovered that she did not die with the others. There was another housekeeper working here that day. This Hilda woman knew what would happen so she skipped out. She was the brains behind everything and planned the showdown that night.

"The entire investigation was clouded by the incredible circumstances. The fact that the Governor was Hilda's brother, and thus Hitler's son, was never revealed. It was done to protect his memory. Consequently, the identity of the housekeeper was never revealed."

"Roy told me that she was definitely Hitler's daughter, but that he may not have been her brother. They were sep-

arated as children, and she just presumed he was her brother," Brad said.

"Anyway," the Governor resumed, "I was the next governor to use this Residence. I found evidence that Hilda
was not the woman who was killed. No one..... and I mean
no one..... knows. I didn't realize the significance until
George told me the truth about what happened the night
that Governor Hansler was killed. I saw a picture of the
dead woman at the scene. Then about a year ago, I found
a clipping from a newspaper that had slipped down behind
the dresser in the room used by the housekeeper. It's in this
drawer."

The Governor opened the drawer and took out the clipping. He handed it to Brad first. It was in the *Chicago
Tribune* on July 10, 1978, and read:

> Yesterday there was a rally in Chicago's Marquette
> Park sponsored by the Nationalist Socialist Party of
> America, a white supremacist organization based on
> Adolph Hitler's Nazi Party. More than 2,000 demon-
> strators congregated in the park shouting racial slurs
> and Nazi slogans. A Supreme Court ruling a month ear-
> lier had been rendered giving them the right to demon-
> strate peaceably. It took 400 police officers to avert a
> riot between the Nazis and the counter-demonstrators.
> Listed among the leaders of the Nazi demonstrators
> were an Emil Schwartz and his daughter, Hilda, pic-
> tured below.

There was a picture of Hilda and her father.

The Governor said, "Of course this Schwartz and his

wife had adopted her when she was five or six years old. They raised her to become a fanatic like her adopted father, because they knew she was Hitler's daughter. Whether the historians believe it or not, there's proof that Hitler had a daughter and a son born in Sweden. It was verified in an article in *Life* magazine back in 1945."

Reino chimed in, "Wait a minute Governor. What does this have to do with why we're here? With Ingra and Jennie getting killed? Or with this threat from ODAM?"

Governor Broadwell was a shrewd man. "Think about it. You know who the Detroit ODAM leader is.... right..... Jacque Kamel. Have you ever heard either Sam or George say who the Chicago leader is? I haven't."

"My gosh," Brad said. "Do you really think that this same Hilda could be the Chicago leader of ODAM, Governor? You would be the only person to figure it out.... because no one else knew that she might still be alive."

"It's a long shot. If she is still alive, she is probably active in some neo-Nazi or other fanatical activity.... and ODAM fits the bill."

"I think you're right, Governor," Reino said. "Do you want Brad and me to tell George and Sam.... or do you want to?"

"Let me stay clear. It's better that way. You two handle the communications and just keep me informed."

Brad said, "I think that's wise Governor. You have contributed a great deal already."

"Thank you. Now Reino. You do as I told you. If you have any trouble.... tell the manager to call me."

It was four o'clock. Reino and Brad excused themselves,

and walked along the top of the hill from the Governor's Residence to the Grand Hotel. Reino knew that Brad would ask him what the Governor's last statement was all about. He told him to wait a few minutes, and he'll find out. Reino flashed his badge at the entrance to the majestic Grand. The young lady didn't hesitate to call Assistant Manager Jake Gibbons for Reino.

"Howdy Jake. I need to see ya right now. Are ya free?"

"Sure, come right in, Reino." The office was around the corner from the registration desk, and past a gift shop.

"We must have a room next to the Chinese Foreign Minister on all the nights he is here, beginning on September eleventh," Reino insisted.

"Do you know how much that will cost?" Jake Gibbons grimaced as he waved both arms upward to indicate the magnitude of the figure.

"The new Conservative Party will pay for it. The Governor promised. It's a legitimate security measure."

Jake looked for a loophole. He was already overbooked, and didn't want to give up the room.

"Won't these congressmen get in trouble by inviting some foreign official to a closed room political meeting?"

Reino countered, "The Governor said that it has been cleared with the Senate Foreign Relations Committee..... or whatever it's called..... and the FBI appointed Sam Green in charge of security."

Outsmarted by Reino, Jake acquiesced and reassigned the room. Reino said, "Let's make up a name. We can't use any name associated with us. How about Gary Dean.... he's an old school chum of mine."

"Thank you, Jake. Either Brad or I will register as Gary Dean. If there is any problem we'll ask for you.... okay?"

"Sure. It'll be a hectic weekend.... a little more won't make a difference," he moaned.

They went upstairs to look at the location of the luxurious suite assigned to the Foreign Minister, and the one that they reserved next door. It was an ultra expensive, but much smaller, suite. They walked back to the main street. Reino took a Star Lines Ferry to St. Ignace, and Brad took the Arnold Catamaran to Mackinaw City.

◯

BRAD STOPPED TO EAT AT DARROW'S RESTAURANT. ONE OF THE waitresses had gone to high school with Brad, and still had a crush on him. She managed to wait on him most of the time, thanks to the cooperation of the other waitresses. Unfortunately.... for her that is.... he was oblivious of her affection. After his usual tossed salad with ranch dressing, to accompany his fried whitefish sandwich, he drove along the lake to the cottage.

The next day, Saturday, he tried to call Sam. He was politely told that Mr. Green was on a case, and couldn't be reached until Monday.

On Saturday night Brad was awakened from a sound sleep by a squeak in the floor boards of his sixty-year-old cottage. He opened his eyes to see something glisten above his head. He instinctively twisted his head as the blade of a long knife plunged down into the pillow. He sprung out of bed, as if he were on a trampoline. The man came at him again. Brad sidestepped just in time as the knife smashed into his picture of the *Stewart J Cort*, the first 1,000-foot laker. It smashed the glass and split the frame in half, particles flying all over the room.

Brad reached for the long black flashlight that he kept beside his bed as the man lunged toward him once more. This time Brad caught a glimpse of the man's face. It was the ghost of Peter Lorre.... right out of *Casablanca*.... he thought. He knew that it was Chang Hai.

Brad managed to swing the heavy flashlight as the knife came at him again. The flashlight hit his arm deflecting the knife away. Chang Hai pushed Brad down, and ran out of the dark bedroom. He ran out the front door, and into the woods in back of the cottages along the lake. He climbed the hill a few hundred feet back and disappeared into the darkness.

Brad ran out on the porch. He was too stunned to try to chase him. The cottage, intended for summer vacationing only, was not built with the protection of the modern city houses. There was little or no crime to be considered back in the good old days. The entrance to the cottage had a French door with twelve small panes of glass. The intruder had merely wedged one of the glass panes out of the molding and reached in for the door knob.

It was after four in the morning. Brad sat up with the lights on until daylight, which came very early, in the month of August. He decided not to alert the local police chief, Wilbert Erbe. He knew why Chang had attacked him. It was not a matter for the police. He couldn't expose the reasons and the implications to anyone except Reino and Sam.

18.

◆ THE *MALAGA BADRA* WAS ON ITS WAY FROM
Honolulu to the Panama Canal and then northward toward the St. Lawrence Seaway. Chang Hai
was on his way from Lansing to Chicago and from there to
Honolulu. He was disgruntled at his failure to dispose of
the evasive professor. He concluded that it was more luck
than brains on the part of the professor. If the floor hadn't
squeaked at the wrong moment.... if he hadn't been so
quick on his feet.

But no one need know about his failure. He would just
tell the good Captain Tan that the elusive professor was
never home.... or that something more urgent came up. And
Chang did not have to explain to anyone else. ODAM had
paid him to complete a mission. They usually didn't care
who had to be eliminated in the process. He had a better
idea how to disable the professor anyway.

His plane landed in Honolulu on Monday afternoon. Chang registered at the Moana Hotel, Waikiki's oldest hotel. It is ironic that Japan never invaded Hawaii after bombing Pearl Harbor, since they now own the three oldest and finest hotels, anyway.

Sure enough, at Chang Hai's request, an ODAM agent had followed Brad when he was in Honolulu for his last classes. He observed his obvious interest in Madelaine, and reported it to Chang before he had departed for Michigan. Chang went to the House Without A Key on Tuesday night.

Madelaine finished her first performance and headed for her dressing room. Chang sat near the aisle in the back. He stood up as she was passing and said, "Miss Kaleo, may I speak with you a moment?"

Madelaine was amused with the resemblance he had with Peter Lorre, or was it Wo Fat, Jack Lord's main adversary in the episodes of "Hawaii Five-O?" The man reached out his hand displaying a wallet with credentials that looked impressive. They were in fact an imitation of those of a law enforcement officer from Kuala Lumpur, Malaysia. Madelaine looked at the credentials and said, "Yes.... what is it?"

"My name is Inspector Jared Mohar, from Kuala Lumpur, as my credentials indicate. I have been looking for a man posing as an American professor. He goes by the name of Bradley Kendall."

Madelaine was inwardly shocked. She tried to hide her emotion.... and did so effectively. She simply said, "Yes?"

"I understand that you know him. Is that true?"

Madelaine wasn't quite sure how to answer.... but she had to make a quick decision.

"There is an American professor with that name who has shown an interest in me. But.... that occurs commonly with someone in my profession."

She stated it nonchalantly. She knew that he wouldn't have asked the question unless he already had some indication that she was more than just casually acquainted with Bradley. Chang knew very well that they had spent time together. His informant had followed them as they drove around Oahu.

He continued his admonition. "I want to warn you that this imposter is a most dangerous agent for an international terrorist group. Do not believe anything he says about his work. He is very convincing. But do not be fooled. Try to avoid him if he attempts to see you again, because he is interested in you only for sex. That is his trademark. He lures beautiful women into his confidence.... and then.... I will not say more."

Chang stopped to watch for her reaction. He had done the damage he intended.... to put doubt in her mind.

"You may have already learned too much about him. And when he tires of your.... I must admit that even I have noticed your tempting feminine qualities.... well.... he is notorious for disposing of his female companions."

Her face could no longer hide her ambivalent feelings. She managed to say, "I.... just can't believe it.... he seemed like such a nice young man."

Poor Madelaine's dreams of her perfect man, the kindly professor, were shattered. She didn't want to believe the

Inspector, but why would he say such a thing if it weren't true?

Chang got up and said, "I must go now. My flight is soon. I just wanted to warn you to be careful. Don't bother to go to Five-O. They won't believe you. This agent is too clever. Good-bye Miss Kaleo."

Chang disappeared quickly before she could ask any questions. He had planted the seed that would make the professor miserable for a while. If and when the professor returned to Hawaii to unravel the mystery of why his lady friend suddenly rejected him, our dear Mr. Chang could more easily arrange for the unfortunate demise of both of them.

Chang Hai had made one serious mistake, however. He assumed that no man could resist the sensual attraction of the beautiful Madelaine. In international circles American men were assumed to have no resistance at all to the lure of a beautiful woman. And Madelaine was the epitome of feminine magnetism. Chang Hai had no doubt that sexual conquest had to be Professor Bradley Kendall's motive for pursuing this Goddess of Love. He would never expect that the scholarly accounting professor, Bradley Kendall, placed more importance on his principles.

This was the one inconsistent description of Bradley that spun around in Madelaine's mind. It gave her some hope.... but not enough to undo the confusion and fear that Chang had injected into her thoughts. Brad's actions did not seem to fit those expected from the man that Chang described. But then.... clever spies were trained to hide their true identity.... she well knew.

Maybe all that goody-goody two shoes business that Brad had displayed as the perfect gentleman, was just an act. He may have needed her for some ominous act that he was going to perform. All kinds of foolish thoughts went through her head.

She tried to remember what Brad had said when he left from the Honolulu Airport in July. Was he coming back to see her.... or didn't he say? Then she remembered, he said that he would be back sooner than she expected. Oh dear!

TUESDAY, AUGUST 25

BRAD WAS READING THE LETTER HE HAD RECEIVED AT THE END of the last semester, in May, from the Academic Vice-President of Lake Superior State University.

"Professor Bradley Kendall has been granted a leave for study during the Fall Semester."

He had received a contract from Quorum Books to write another book on Activity Based Costing (ABC), and was in the midst of gathering research material for it. One of the companies he planned to use for his case studies was in Honolulu, and another was in Penang, Malaysia.

The City of Honolulu had become interested in the new cost management principles in his articles and in his first book. They had instituted a new activity-based costing system designed for non-profit government agencies two years ago. Also, in Penang, a division of the American company, Advanced Micro Devices, the maker of semiconductors, had innovated an activity-based costing system that was an ideal model for the research study.

He could make his own timetable, and this was a good

time to complete the case study in Honolulu. The fact that he could see Madelaine again was a fringe benefit. He knew that he would have to go sometime during the next three or four months when he told Madelaine that he might return sooner than she might expect. He decided to wait and surprise her at the House Without A Key rather than let her know that he was coming.

He called the travel agency in Cheboygan and made a reservation for Thursday to fly to Honolulu. He called Reino. "Allo Reino.... This is...."

"Don't say it. Hello there Brad, ol' boy. I'd know your poor excuse for a Finglish accent anytime."

"Just wanted you to know that I'm flying out of here for Honolulu on Thursday, old pal."

"You pronounced it wrong. You mean for Hokulani don't you? Isn't that Madelaine's Hawaiian name?"

"Is it that obvious, old buddy? I tried to keep it a secret, you know. Seriously though, I do have to go there.... for the research leave. Did I tell you about it?"

"Sure. You told me a coupla months ago. What's all this research stuff about, anyway? Isn't it just a way to get a free trip to Hawaii?"

"It could be.... but, not in my case. Earlier this year, a financial manager for the City of Indianapolis reviewed my most recent book on activity-based costing. Then the City of Honolulu Finance Director offered to pay me as a consultant to analyze their newly-installed ABC system adapted to governmental accounting. I told him that I would accept travel expenses, but no consulting fee. I suggested that if I could use his new system as one of my case studies, it would be mutually beneficial. I don't believe in milking the system. I'm paid well by a tax-supported university to be a professor and to do research. In my opinion it would be double-dipping to charge a fee."

"I heard that the professors at the big name colleges spend more time and make more money on consulting than they do from their salaries." Reino queried.

"Some do.... even some accounting professors.... I am sure. In my experience though, the professors at most universities tend to be very ethical in their relations with the business world."

Reino decided to get back to the real world with the conversation. "Do you need a ride to the airport?"

"No. I'll drive to Lansing. I want to talk to Sam before I leave. Would you contact him for me and ask him to give me a call?"

Brad knew that it was easier for Reino, a sheriff, to get through to the head of the FBI in Detroit. Sometimes Brad had trouble getting through to him. Sam was so often on high priority missions.

Reino said, "Can you meet me for lunch tomorrow, say at twelve-thirty at Anna's Buffet? I like the food there. They have lots to eat!"

"Okay. See you then."

On Wednesday they met at Anna's Country Buffet on Huron Street. Reino and Brad hurried to get in the line before a tour bus unloaded its hungry passengers. It was not difficult to identify them as senior citizens. As soon as the colleges began their fall classes, the senior citizen tour bus season began. A second bus was unloading its passengers at the Admiral's Table, across the street.

"Reino, do you remember my mentor and friend, Roy Nelson?"

"Sure. He's your professor friend whose wife was killed in that terrible plane crash in Detroit a few years back. Then he married the Hawaiian girl. Governor Broadwell mentioned that he was involved with that tragedy on Mackinac Island .... when Governor Hansler and what's-er-name were supposed to have been killed."

"You mean Hilda Schwartz. Governor Broadwell told us that she is probably still alive. Anyway.... what I was going to tell you was that I am going to ask Roy to help me on the research project. After he married the Hawaiian girl, Luana, he applied for a position as an accounting professor at the University of Hawaii."

"I remember," Reino added. "You told me that his family had a cottage along Lakeside Drive. He worked for George and the INS on that Hilda thing, didn't he?"

"Yes. By the way, did you get in touch with Sam for me, Reino?"

"Yes," Reino said. "He said he would be at Clara's at noon, like you asked. Okay? Now remember.... when you get to Hawaii make sure that you ask George exactly what he wants us to do. You and Sam and I are probably going to have to coordinate the game plan.... or whatever ya call it!"

"Right, I'll be talking to Sam tomorrow. Thanks for calling him for me. And I'll get in touch with George as soon as

I get over there. He always wants me to touch base. Especially with a project as crucial as this one."

After they both stuffed themselves with the tasty selection of food on the buffet, Reino drove back to St. Ignace, and Brad went to the cottage.

19.

THE NEXT DAY BRAD WAS ON HIS WAY TO LANSING. HE met the FBI's illustrious Sam Green at Clara's, now a museum-like restaurant in the original Michigan Central Railroad Station, built in 1903.

"Have you heard anything new from George?" Brad asked.

"I've been swamped with cases recently. I haven't had time to call George. I told my assistant to always let me know when either he or Reino calls. I've been making arrangements for the September meetings on the Island, too. That gets first priority."

"Okay. I'll be in Hawaii tonight, and will probably see George within the next couple days. If there's anything new, I'll let you know when I get back. Of course, he'll let you know himself if it's something urgent. Let's see, my plane leaves in forty-five minutes. I'll see you in about two weeks, Sam."

O

BRAD TOOK OFF FROM THE LANSING AIRPORT AT TWO-THIRTY-
five. He arrived in Honolulu shortly after eight o'clock that
evening, rented his Alamo Buick LeSabre, and drove down
Nimitz Highway to Ala Moana Boulevard. He passed the
Aloha Tower, Fort DeRussy, and turned on Kalakaua
Avenue to the Royal Hawaiian Hotel. By the time he
arrived at the hotel it was nearly ten o'clock Honolulu time.
That was four a.m. in Michigan daylight savings time. He
fell asleep the moment his head touched the pillow.

Brad woke up at eight on Friday morning. He was looking forward to the fabulous breakfast buffet at the Royal
Hawaiian. After his immersion into the world of delectable
morsels from both Occidental and Oriental cultures, Brad
returned to the room and called his professor friend, Roy
Nelson, at the University of Hawaii- Manoa campus.

Roy answered at his office on campus. "Hello Brad, I
haven't heard from you for awhile."

"Am I glad to catch you in. I need help on a research
project. It won't interfere with your schedule, and will not
take much time. I mainly need you as a second opinion.
Can we get together so I can explain it?"

"How about tomorrow? Luana will be at her mother's
house in Kailua all day."

"Thanks, Roy. Would you mind if we go out to the
Arizona Memorial? I haven't been there for a long time."

On Friday afternoon Brad drove to the Punch Bowl. The
national cemetery located on the side of a dormant crater
was the final resting place of more than twenty thousand

Americans, mainly veterans of the Pacific region battles. The contemplation of Punch Bowl and the *Arizona* Memorial was important to Brad. The visual observance of these two sacred cemeteries helped him to acknowledge the supreme sacrifice made by these American veterans.

The next morning Roy met Brad at the only Big Boy in Honolulu, which was on the way to Pearl Harbor. You wouldn't find some of their menu selections at any of the Big Boys in the Midwest.

They drove to the Pearl Harbor *Arizona* Memorial Visitors Center, next to the Naval Base. The visitors were separated into groups waiting to board a ferry, operated by the U.S. Navy, which took them to the site of the sunken *Arizona*. The groups that were waiting to board were invited to listen to a talk, and to see a movie about the Memorial.

More than one-half of the visitors were Japanese tourists. The guide was in the process of telling the group that a few days ago one of the Japanese tourists said that he was a captain of one of the two-man submarines that entered the harbor to torpedo the American ships.

Roy nostalgically recalled, "My first wife, Eleanor, came here with me in 1988. When she first saw the Japanese tourists, she became sick with a pent-up hatred from her childhood. We were old enough to remember the hatred of the soldiers who were killing our American boys. Younger people can't really understand what it was like to live through World War II. When Eleanor was on the Memorial she deliberately walked up to a Japanese tourist, old enough to have fought in the war, smiled politely at him, and shook his hand. After that she was all right."

Brad remembered that Eleanor was killed in a plane crash in 1991, and that they had three sons who would now be in their late twenties. Roy still talked about her a lot.... but not when Luana was around.

"I can understand how older Americans must feel about Pearl Harbor. I have no use for those Americans who criticize us for bombing Hiroshima and Nagasaki," Brad opined.

"The facts are that we saved half a million American lives, and at least two million Japanese lives. My father told me many times that I would probably not be alive if it weren't for the atomic bombs. He joined the army as soon as he was eighteen, and was in training for the invasion. Japanese women and children were trained to fight to the death when the Americans invaded their land. I have no doubt that it would have been a slaughter. And the two atomic bombs did not kill nearly as many people as our conventional bombs did."

Roy added, "And it showed the world how terrible a nuclear war could be. It prevented a nuclear war for more than fifty years."

When their group was ferried out to the *Arizona* Memorial Brad noticed a drop of oil rising to the surface from the hull of the sunken *Arizona*. The guide explained to the tourists, "Those drops of oil have been coming to the surface for the past fifty-six years. It has varied, but they are now about one minute apart."

To Brad there was nothing so intense as when you stood

on top of this sunken battleship with the bodies of more than eleven hundred American sailors below. Although he had been here twice before, he needed to reinforce, just for himself, the importance of remembering the sacrifice that our veterans have made.

Roy pointed to the large circle where one of the big-gun turrets had been. "I told you about the turret, didn't I Brad?"

"Yes. You told me the story of how the turret and big guns were barged over to Kaneohe and dug into Ulupau Crater, along with only one machine gun nest."

"But did you know that the Japanese bombed Pearl Harbor on December eighth?"

Brad stopped to think a moment. "No, but it just dawned on me. It would be the next day in Tokyo because of the International Date Line. You're right.... in Japan it would be the eighth, not the seventh of December."

"Now, what did you want me to do for your research project, Bradley?"

"I would like you to come with me when I first visit the City of Honolulu's Finance Director, James Tanaka. He told me that you two were friends. You know more about governmental accounting than I do, so I would like your observations about their newly-installed ABC system. Nothing formal, but I want you to be the devil's advocate. Whenever you spot a weakness in the system, tear it to pieces. Tanaka and I will have to explain and defend the practice. That way I'll be more confident that it is really necessary."

"That doesn't sound too hard," Roy expressed. "In fact, it should be fun. Just let me know when. I'll give you a copy of my class schedule and office hours so you can find an open time. Give me a call."

Brad said, "Too many practitioners defend practices for personal ego reasons. They spend money on a failed project, and then hang on to it because they don't want to admit they made a mistake."

"I agree, Brad. And too many companies waste money on consultants. How can a company justify hiring a management consultant to give advice to managers? They are paid to manage. If they don't know how, they should be fired. Every college business major has been inundated with accounting, management, marketing, and finance courses. I admit subjects like accounting and engineering are technical, but management is ninety percent common sense."

After the emotional tour of the *Arizona*, and a few more philosophical tirades, the two friendly academicians, Brad and Roy, walked out to the parking lot. They located their cars and parted.

○

BRAD DROVE STRAIGHT TO THE ROYAL HAWAIIAN. HE WAS becoming anxious to go to the House Without A Key and see sweet, adorable Madelaine. It was Saturday. She would be dancing tonight, and he would surprise her. She would be so delighted to see him. He couldn't believe that it was over six weeks since they were together. He remembered how she kissed him gently on both cheeks, Hawaiian style.... and how he gave her a hug, Bradley style, spontaneous and clumsy.

At eight o'clock he walked from the Royal Hawaiian to the Polynesian Hotel. He knew she took her last break at eight-thirty. He could visit with her for a while, and then watch the entertainment until it ended at nine-thirty.

The House Without A Key was almost full on Saturday night. Brad found a table way in the back and ordered a cup of coffee and a croissant. Madelaine was dancing to the soothing Hawaiian music. At her break she walked to the back of the restaurant toward her dressing room. She spotted Brad on the other side waving his arm at her. Her heart pounded. What should she do? She couldn't ignore him, and she couldn't run.... like she wanted to. She walked slowly toward him.

"Hello Mr. Kendall. Are you here on business again?"

Brad was jolted. What a cold reception! He didn't understand why.... except.... he just realized. He didn't even call her in six weeks. She must be upset with him because of that.... what else?

"Madelaine, the name is Brad, and I'm sorry I didn't call you. I wanted to surprise you. I thought you'd be...."

Madelaine interrupted him, "I'm so sorry, Mr. Kendall.

I must go now and get ready for my next show. It was nice to see you again."

She walked away to her dressing room briskly, leaving Brad with his mouth open, ready to say something.... but what? At the end of the show Madelaine whisked away to the back without as much as peeking in Brad's direction. Brad stood up and looked around for her, but she had disappeared. One of the musicians told Brad that she left without saying a word to anyone, which was very unusual.

Brad walked back to the Royal Hawaiian, watched an old "Hawaii Five-O" movie, the late news, and went to bed wondering what he had done wrong with Madelaine. He was not very astute when it came to women. He assumed that he had blundered again. He liked Madelaine. He had liked Jennie, too. Why was he so clumsy with women? Were all accounting professors so timid and naïve around them? Chances are she doesn't really like him, and wants to avoid him. After all.... she's a beautiful girl, and he's just an ordinary fellow.

It was Monday before he could see her again. He was afraid to call on her at her home, considering the reception he got, but he could certainly go to watch her dance. He had a sumptuous buffet lunch at the Surf Room in the Royal Hawaiian. He didn't like to have a big meal at night, and he wanted to sit and eat snacks at the House Without A Key while he watched Madelaine dance. He walked over early to make sure that he would have more time to find out why she acted so strangely.

He spotted Ben Shirakawa, the sexagenarian guitar player, who was practicing with Sam Akaka and the other member of the trio. They were on the stage, which was up front by the ocean. Ben had always been very friendly with Brad when he came to see Madelaine.

"Do you know what happened to Madelaine, Ben? She wasn't happy to see me this time. She acted as if she didn't know me. Did she say anything to you?"

"You mean Hokulani? That's what we call her. Not a thing. I thought she was crazy about you.... the way she was so happy when you was here last July. But then.... there was a guy here.... let's see.... it was about a week ago. Ever since he talked to her, she has been moody.... an' kinda.... scared lookin'."

"What did he look like? Did you notice?"

"Well.... now that you mention it.... he kinda looked like that old actor in *Casablanca*.... you know who I mean?"

"Peter Lorre?"

"That's the guy. He was a cross between him and Hawaii Five-O's Wo Fat.... remember him? They're still showing 'Five-O' reruns on the TV."

Brad preached analytical skills in his accounting classes. He had switched to open book exams to emphasize comprehending, rather than memorizing, the principles and problems. He needed to apply those skills right now. That bastar' sorry.... buggar, Chang Hai.... had scared her. But how? Chang had made her afraid of him. He must have lied about something. Brad had to find out.

"Ben, when is Madelaine, I mean Hokulani, coming in? I need to see her before the show."

"Oh.... I'm sorry professor, I forgot to tell you that Hokulani won't be dancing tonight. She was asked to pose for a travel magazine advertiser today. They have been up at the Pali Lookout most of the afternoon. She told me that they wanted some pictures in the daylight, and some at dusk with moonlight. So we have a substitute dancer tonight."

"Thanks Ben. I'll see you later if, and when, I find out what's eating your Hokulani, or whatever her name is."

Brad practically ran back to the Royal Hawaiian and to the fifth floor of the parking garage where his trusty Buick rental car was parked. He drove down Ali Wai Canal Street, and then down McCully, over to King Street. He passed by the old location of King's Bakery and restaurant. How he had loved to have breakfast with the local Hawaiian people. It was one of the few places where he could enjoy the local Hawaiian people without having tourists around.

Why did they have to close King's, and the beautiful Canlis Restaurant; and then the exquisite Willows, where they served Poi, and the kanes, the wahines, and the tutu's would spontaneously get up and dance the hula at the urging of their friends? At least he still had Maple Garden, with Robert at the cash register. He hoped that the tourists hadn't yet discovered this unique and truly Chinese restaurant with local Hawaiian flavor.

He drove to downtown Honolulu, and onto the Pali Highway, which cuts over and through the Koolau Mountains from Honolulu to Kailua and Kaneohe. At the top, just before the tunnel, is the Nuuanu Pali Lookout, a tourist attraction overlooking the windward towns and bays and Mt. Olomano.

Brad pulled off at the tourist drive, which ascended to the Lookout. The Pali Lookout is situated at edge of a cliff, the site of the 1795 battle in which King Kamehameha I vanquished his opponents, and conquered Oahu in his quest to unite the Hawaiian Islands. His soldiers literally pushed the defending army over the cliff to the rocks hundreds of feet below.

It was six-thirty and starting to get dark. A large van was parked near the entrance to the tourist area The last time Brad visited the Pali Lookout the wind was too strong to stand up straight. He had to stoop over in order to walk to the edge. He facetiously wondered why the Hawaiian soldiers who were forced off the cliff didn't just float safely away by the force of the powerful winds.

The visitors area consisted of a stepped, walled platform made of poured concrete, with a sturdy iron fence circling the edge of the cliff. The tourists could see as far as Mokapu Point at the end of the Kaneohe Marine Air Corps Station, and up the coast to Chinaman's Hat.

The wind was not quite as strong as it had been on his earlier visit. The name of the tourist magazine, *Pacific Travel*, was printed on the side of the van. Two men and a woman were loading equipment on the van.

"Hello there. Is Madelaine here?"

The woman, who looked more like a Swede than a Hawaiian, pointed. "Oh! She's still over there. She wanted to say a few prayers for her ancestors. Hawaiians are funny that way.... don't ya know! Tell her we're leaving now. She has her own car."

Brad said thank you, and walked toward the rail. He looked back and saw the van drive off. He saw Madelaine standing at the rail with her head down, and her hands clasped together in front of her.

"Madelaine. Hi! It's me Brad. I want to talk to you."

Madelaine turned around and saw Brad. She ran to the left, and down a flight of iron stairs. In her fright she forgot that it led to a small lower level lookout balcony. The only way out, other than the stairway, was the same way that King Kamehameha's enemies went, over the cliff. As Brad descended the stairway and stepped onto the small balcony a few feet away from her, she shuddered with fear. She quickly said a prayer, for herself, instead of her ancestors.

"Madelaine, why are you afraid? It's me, Brad. I would never hurt you in a million years."

She remembered the warning of that Inspector Jared Mohar, from Kuala Lumpur. Don't believe anything he says. He is trained to dispose of anyone who gets in his way. She was too frightened to speak.

Brad, finally realizing the extreme intensity of her fear, tried to imagine what that monster Chang Hai had told her. He had to convince her that he, not Chang, was telling the truth.

"Madelaine, listen carefully. I know that a man went to see you. He must have scared you terribly. I don't know how, but I can guess. Stop and think. When I returned from Singapore I told you that I was kidnapped on the *Malaga Badra*. I told you that the first mate was Chang Hai, one of the leaders of ODAM. He's the one who killed Ingra Jensen. He tried to kill me again in Mackinaw. I was going to tell you all about it the other night, but.... you seemed frightened and ran away from me. I didn't know why. If he said that I was some kind of an imposter, it was just to get even with me for escaping his attempt to kill me. It must have made him furious. And he figured that if he convinced you that I was a.... I don't know what.... but, some kind of an imposter maybe.... well.... then you wouldn't trust me .... or something like that."

Brad stopped to observe Madelaine's reaction. "This is important. If he looked a little like Peter Lorre or Wo Fat, then you should know that the man who talked to you was Chang Hai."

At that, Madelaine remembered her first impression of the man who looked like Wo Fat. Her face glowed. She practically leaped into Brad's arms. She hugged him as the tears ran profusely down her cheeks.

"Oh I'm so sorry.... so sorry. Why did I believe him? I should have believed in you Bradley. He confused me. He had credentials.... and said you were an imposter.... some kind of an international terrorist. He said you would kill me if I found out. Oh, how stupid I was to believe him. Please forgive me."

She kissed him, and hugged him, and kissed him again and again, not on the cheeks this time. She squeezed him so tight that her voluptuous body neutralized every single one of his internal and external defense mechanisms against the invasion of female irresistibility.

"Oh.... I'm so sorry. I couldn't help myself." She apologized for her unlady-like behavior.

Brad didn't mind a bit. He continued to hold her tight. "You never have to worry about me again, Madelaine." Then he laughed. "It was all just a plan to get you to hug me!"

"Oh you...." She hugged him again, while he melted into a state of Nirvana, or whatever that kind of temptation is called. After recovering from the shock of this confusion, they returned to their cars and drove to Madelaine's beach house in Waimanalo. They both had such an exhausting day, they relaxed on the porch watching the waves splash on the shore. The full moon lit up the sky, making the blue water glisten.

"Do you believe in Madame Pele?" Brad surprisingly asked.

Madelaine pondered a moment before answering. "I'm probably over one-half, almost three-quarters Hawaiian, although it's not easy to determine what a pure bred Hawaiian really is any more. My mother named me Madelaine deliberately, so I wouldn't be stereotyped as a native. My grandmother wanted my first name to be Hokulani. So they compromised. Now I use Hokulani when I teach the Waimanalo school children the Hawaiian chants and dances, and when I dance at the House Without A Key at the Polynesian Hotel."

She continued, "I almost have to believe in Pele, Bradley. It doesn't matter whether my rational mind believes or not. All that matters is that my heart, which is the cultural or ancestral part of me has to believe. My grandmother believed. My mother believes.... about the same way I do. I have no choice."

"How about your father?"

"He's not convinced, probably because his parents were not believers."

"It might be similar to my believing in Santa Claus. I know he's not real. I know that it's impossible for him to drop off presents to millions of homes in one night. But, I still want to believe in Santa Claus. What would our child-hood be like without him? Children love the reindeer, the elves, the red suit, and even the whiskers. It's a tradition. We love it."

"That's close to our love for Pele. I want to believe in her because I love the legend. It's nostalgic and comforting to me. But, I don't worship Pele as a God, only as a tradition."

"Just wondered," Brad closed the discussion. It was almost eleven o'clock when he excused himself to go to the hotel.

Madelaine's eyes twinkled a bit as she surprisingly offered, "You know that you don't have to stay in the hotel while you're here. You can stay right here in my house. I have an extra bedroom."

Brad's surprise was not obscure.

"I don't mean.... that is.... it's not what it sounds like, Bradley. I wouldn't say that to anyone else. I know what a gentleman you are. So I wouldn't worry about.... you know.... those things that girls have to worry about."

Brad wasn't sure that was a compliment for a macho man. But he wasn't a macho man anyway.

"Thank you for the compliment, Madelaine. I'd better not. I wouldn't want anyone to question your integrity. You and I know the truth, but other people would assume otherwise. And it will be fun to visit you, more like courting."

Ye gads, what did he commit himself to, without thinking? Courting sounds like going steady. He lived in Michigan, not Hawaii. How was he going to court her?

20.

IT WAS TIME TO SEE GEORGE. BRAD CALLED HIM AT THE Kahana and arranged to have breakfast in the small gazebo-shaped dining room used for large parties, or by the local businesses for meetings. The entire restaurant was surrounded by water colorfully occupied by the large goldfish, actually carp, that were so cherished by the Japanese. With the goldfish and a waterfall placed in the oriental setting, the Kahana made a splendid place to relax and enjoy the food. Brad didn't know why the pancakes tasted so good there. Maybe it was just psychological. He loved the Poor Boy Special. It had a fried egg, over easy, on top of two delicious pancakes, with two slices of thick bacon. With pure maple syrup poured over the pancakes, the Poor Boy made Brad very rich in terms of satisfaction.

George Tong, owner of the Kahana, met him in the private room after Brad had eaten.

"I already had breakfast at seven-thirty so I thought I would let you enjoy yours before we talked."

"Thank you, George. I enjoy your food too much to spoil it with conversation.... especially as important as ours."

George became serious. "We have much new information, Bradley. One of the main items on the agenda of the new Conservative Party's Strategy meeting is to begin the campaign to promote Paul Bunche, Governor of Texas, for President in the year 2000. We have even more reason to be concerned about the meeting on Mackinac Island."

"Why is that, George?"

"Paul Bunche, has more influence with the Chinese Foreign Minister, Chong Lo Pan, because of his father, who knew most of the current leaders, and had their respect. If Paul Bunche is elected president, there will be a greater chance of cooperation between the U.S. and mainland China. The ODAM leaders are determined to cause a rift in this friendship."

"You mean, George, that the ODAM leaders don't want cooperation between our two nations?"

"Yes, and now I have good news. We have been able to place an experienced INS member in the ODAM secret council. He goes by the name of Kochark. Don't tell anyone about him, except Sam Green and Reino. He attended his first meeting back in July. He had to wait for a safe way to contact me about the meeting. I just received his message two weeks ago. The meeting was in Bangkok. The leader of ODAM is a man called Sauloo. It cost us ten million U.S. dollars to join the group, but we will get the money back....when this is all over, of course."

George waved to a waitress, "Do you want more coffee, Bradley?"

"Yes, thank you, George."

"Meylia, would you please bring us more coffee and a pot of tea.... you know what kind, for me."

George continued as the coffee and tea were being delivered. "Kochark reported that there were four other ODAM members present. One of them was Chang Hai. He reported that his position as first mate on the *Malaga Badra* was a way to give him mobility in and out of foreign countries. Jacque Kamel in Detroit reports to Chang Hai."

"Did he mention who is the head of the Chicago ODAM operation?" Brad asked.

"No, except that Sauloo once used the word, she, when he referred to the Chicago operation."

"Now I have something to report to you, George," Brad said, with a tone of importance in his voice. "Reino and I had a meeting with Governor Broadwell about two weeks ago on Mackinac Island. He told us that Hilda Schwartz might still be alive."

"But Hilda was reported killed in the shootout with the others."

"Governor Broadwell has evidence, which he found in the Governor's Residence on Mackinac Island, that indicates she was not the woman who was killed. A housekeeper was killed, but it was not Hilda. The Governor said he has never told anyone, except Reino and me. He didn't realize the significance until the question about the Chicago leader of ODAM came up. Now he thinks the leader is Hilda."

"I see.... because why else would her identity be kept a secret, even in the ODAM meetings. Kochark mentioned Jacque Kamel in Detroit, but never the name of the Chicago leader. I believe you and the Governor are right, Bradley."

"I thought you should know, George, because she is a ruthless character. She is certain to surface before long."

"I'll start working on it. Kochark will be traveling to Michigan for the Mackinac Island meeting. He told Sauloo that he wanted to insure that his ten million dollars was well spent. So he made a reservation at the Grand Hotel. Right now he is certain that they plan on disposing of the Chinese foreign minister. He should know all the details of the attack by the time he gets there. He'll use the name Edgar Kozar from Bangkok. I want Sam to contact him, but warn him to be careful not to expose Kochark's connection with us. It would be fatal if he were discovered by Chang Hai or Jacque Kamel."

"Okay, George. You can contact me through Sam's office, or direct to the cottage. I have made certain that no one can intercept our conversations. We'll be ready when the *Malaga Badra* sails under the Mackinac Bridge next week. I know that Sam has been making plans to welcome them to the Island."

Bradley and George soon parted company. It was time to take care of the research project. Brad called Roy Nelson at the University of Hawaii, and then made an appointment with the City of Honolulu's Finance Director, James Tanaka. The appointment was for the next day, Wednesday, September second.

Professor Bradley Kendall and his mentor, Professor Roy

Nelson, observed the activity-based costing system that the City of Honolulu had innovated into its governmental system. Some activities were different from those of the standard manufacturing or marketing company, but the principles were the same. The main difference is profit versus surplus. In governmental accounting profits and losses are euphemistically called surpluses and deficits. It just sounds better.

In Jimmy Carter's days the zero based budgeting idea was introduced. Roy recalled that the Dean of Business at a state university told him in 1970 that he had to purchase a room full of office machines for fifty thousand dollars. He didn't want them or need them, but the budgeting system would automatically reduce their next year's budget allotment if the department didn't spend the money before the end of the fiscal year.

Zero based budgeting eliminated this type of problem by not starting from last year's budget figure, but from zero. It forced all budget units to justify their requests. The politicians torpedoed the Zero, just like the Zeros torpedoed the ships at Pearl Harbor, thought Roy in one of his impish moments.

Brad was satisfied with the results of their interview and observations. The three men had many a verbal fencing match over some of the questionable methods of not-for-profit systems, but all were good natured squabbles. Brad excused Roy at the appropriate time and completed the case study himself.

○

Madelaine. "Come in Bradley. I made you some malasadas. Billy told me that you always stopped at the bakery on Kapahulu Street to get some. They are the best there. Mine won't be as good, but they're homemade."

Just the smell of fresh malasadas, a delicate fried doughnut, served hot, and covered with grains of sugar, put Brad in seventh heaven. Madelaine served them with a cup of Kona coffee.

"Madelaine, I have to go back to Mackinaw right away. I'd love to stay longer, but the big moment is coming next week. I told you a little about it. We have a lot of work to do before the Conservative Party strategy meetings on the Island. After that is all over maybe we can get together again."

Madelaine's eyes twinkled. "I have an idea. I don't mind helping Ben Shirakawa at the House Without A Key out once in a while, but I need a break. Would you mind if I went to Michigan? I have never been in the Midwest. I have heard so much about the Great Lakes and Mackinac. It would be a vacation for me. You can recommend a motel for me. I would be on my own."

She said it all in one breath as if she had to do it quickly. There was complete silence for a few seconds that seemed like minutes.

"Wee-lll.... say something Mr. Professor!"

"Sorry.... I was just thinking. The situation is critical, in terms of.... you know.... what might happen. I don't want you to be in any danger."

"Haven't I heard that song before?" Madelaine joked. "That's the same thing you told me the last time you went back. And then I didn't hear from you for six weeks."

"You're right. But this time I can't take a chance. I promise you that the moment after I am sure there is no more danger, I will personally come back here and escort you over to Mackinac for a vacation. I have to be sure the danger has passed. I don't want you to end up like Jennie. You're much safer here in your own backyard.... so to speak."

"All right killjoy. I know what you mean, though. I might be in the way. And I don't want to take up your time when Sam and Reino need you."

"Thank you for understanding, Madelaine. I know that they will need me when the big weekend begins. And I just can't be worrying about you. Besides, it's only Thursday and my plane doesn't leave until Monday. Are you free tomorrow for lunch?"

"Of course, I'm free while you're still here."

"Let's go to that tea house. You know the one. Up the hill in Manoa, next to the wedding chapel," Brad chuckled. "Isn't it the.... Waimea.... or something.... Tea Room, or Tea House. I don't remember the name exactly, but Hemingway was said to have loved it, and did some of his writing there."

"I know.... but I can't remember the name either," Madelaine confessed.

Brad continued, "Anyway, when I was having lunch

there, two long black limousines pulled up, and parked in front of a small wedding chapel next door. A Japanese bride and groom, and a minister stepped out of one limousine, and three Hawaiian musicians hopped out of the other. They all went into the chapel, and thirty minutes later they all ran out and jumped into the two limousines."

Brad stopped long enough to think about how he loved their grilled mahi-mahi and rice.

"Anyway.... five or ten minutes later one very long white limousine drove up and parked in front of the chapel. Then another Japanese bride and groom, the minister, who could have been the same one for all I know, one Hawaiian guitarist, and one Hawaiian hula dancer, stepped out. Thirty minutes later they scampered out just like the first group. The bride was holding her bouquet of flowers while the guitarist and the hula dancer were throwing rice all over them."

"I know all about it," Madelaine laughed. "The weddings in Japan are supposed to cost twenty or thirty thousand dollars because of their elaborate customs. So, because the Japanese love the Islands for vacations, a whole new industry of wedding chapels developed in Hawaii. They advertise a complete wedding package to the Japanese. The couple can have a Hawaiian wedding, which includes air travel, hotel, and all other fees for about five or six thousand dollars. There are literally hundreds of Japanese couples here every week. Just look along Kalakaua Avenue in Waikiki."

Brad said, "I know. I've seen them. And they're all dressed alike. The young women wear a black short skirt, with a short-sleeved white blouse, and the men wear long black trousers, with a long-sleeved white shirt. By the way, Madelaine, when I finished my lunch, which took one hour or so, two weddings took place, and the third one, another long white limousine, was arriving just as I drove off. What a production line!"

Brad and Madelaine had lunch at, what they both found out was renamed, the Menahune Tea Room, on Friday, and observed a Japanese wedding, only one that day, from their table on the patio. Brad had their delicious special, teriyaki chicken and mahi mahi with rice pilaf, while Madelaine had the Hawaiian ono, a sweet delicate white fish.

On Saturday afternoon they went to the annual junior Hula Contest at the Blaisdell Convention Center in downtown Honolulu. Several of Madelaine's protégés from the Tutu program at the Waimanalo grade school were competing in the contest.

Later they deliberately walked down Kalakaua Avenue and looked for the Japanese newlyweds. "There's number nine," Brad spurted out, as he pointed to another young couple conspicuously dressed in black and white.

"My mother always told me not to point, Bradley. I'm not your mother.... thank heavens.... but please don't point! They might be sensitive."

"That's funny, Madelaine. My mother told me that, too. She scolded me because I always forgot, and pointed at people without thinking. And I'm sure glad you're not my mother.... for lots of reasons."

On Sunday they both found it difficult to face the

inevitable. They agreed that Madelaine should not go to the airport to see him off. They both knew that they might expose their true emotions, and neither was ready for that yet.

21.

◆ ON MONDAY PROFESSOR BRADLEY KENDALL FLEW
out of Honolulu on a United flight to Chicago. He
hopped on a United Express flight to Lansing,
where he located his 1990 Mercedes Benz 300 in the parking lot. It was the first Monday in September. Brad had
completely forgotten that it was Labor Day, and that meant
the famous Bridge Walk in Mackinac.

By the time he had arrived in Lansing it was already
Tuesday morning. It was a cool September day in
Michigan, far from the warm tropical air of Hawaii. He
stopped at the Sugar Bowl in Gaylord for lunch, and at
Ken's Village Market in Indian River for groceries.

At last, at three o'clock, he arrived in Mackinaw City,
still busy with cars and people. Many of the sixty thousand
tourists had already left town after the Mackinac Bridge
Walk, but the motels were always busy during September

and October. The fall was becoming increasingly more popular as a tourist attraction.

○

THE *MALAGA BADRA* HAD ARRIVED AT CHICAGO ON SUNDAY.
The ship always spent two days there while the cargo was
being unloaded. It gave the crew a chance to unwind after
the long ocean voyage. Chang Hai boarded the ship on
Monday. He always seemed to appear out of nowhere. He
and Captain Tan Wo Lin were in the pilothouse talking.

"Mr. Chang, good to see you. What are the orders?"

"You are to depart from here in time to arrive at
Mackinac on Friday night. Our associate, Jacque Kamel,
has a room, under an assumed name, of course, at the
Grand Hotel. I have selected two of our agents to leave the
ship. Jacque owns a Chris-Craft cabin cruiser, which is
berthed in the Mackinac Island Marina. He will meet the
ship at midnight. They have the equipment, which fits into
two large bags or suitcases."

Captain Tan Wo Lin said, "And the two men can drop
down into the launch on a Jacob's ladder, much like the
lake pilots do. I will have it ready."

"Thank you my dear Captain. One cannot enter the
Grand Hotel at midnight unnoticed. So I have reserved a
room for them at the Mission Point Resort, which has an
accessible entrance. On Saturday they will inconspicuous-
ly go straight to their room at the Grand, which is already
reserved for them."

"What is the equipment you refer to, Mr. Chang?"

"The Iraqi member of ODAM has provided us with the

latest weapon they have developed. Why do you think that Saddam stopped the United Nations Inspection team for several weeks? It was because they were just days away from completing this weapon for us. It is a chemical bomb that will kill everyone in the building. The bomb explodes and spreads the deadly chemical throughout the area. The size has been diminished substantially, otherwise it would kill everyone on Mackinac Island."

"I should hope that would not be necessary." Captain Tan didn't mind Chang's individual murder, or political assassination, here and there, but he did not want to be part of a massacre.

"It will be set to go off when Chong Lo Pan is speaking at the Saturday night banquet. Governor Paul Bunche of Texas, who is being promoted by the most influential conservative leaders to be the next president, will be present. It will not only destroy the conservative leadership in America, but will infuriate the Chinese, if we can blame it on domestic terrorists."

"Doesn't any American agency like the CIA or the FBI know about ODAM?"

"No. Only our mysterious adversary in Hawaii has surfaced to challenge us. This professor and his friends seem to suspect that the newspaper woman was killed on our ship, but that does not mean they know about our present mission."

"Do you think he works for the Hawaiian group?" Captain Tan asked.

"Perhaps he does. Or he might have just wanted to find his girlfriend. He said she was his girlfriend. It is more likely that he was lying, and he is an agent for the Hawaiian group."

Chang continued, "He must be destroyed along with his friends. We cannot take a chance that our plan will be exposed."

"How will you find him?"

"I have traced him back to Mackinaw City. He used his true name on the flight reservations. This professor cannot be a professional spy. He makes too many foolish mistakes!"

"Are you traveling with us to Mackinac on Friday?"

"No, my good captain. I have rented an automobile and will take care of a few matters before you arrive. The two agents who depart will be taken by Jacque to their room at the Mission Point Resort. I do not expect to be there."

"Who will place the chemical bomb, or whatever it is, in the room? That may be difficult."

"Jacque Kamel has provided us with drawings of the rooms. The agent, named Patrick Shannon, who is the most skilled for the assignment, was provided by the IRA. He connected the bomb more quickly and accurately than any of the others. He convinced me that it would be safer if only one, or at most, two agents should go to the Island. The bomb is small enough for one man to handle. I selected one other man to assist him. The one who was next most qualified is an Iraqi named Anwar."

"I will not see you again, Mr. Chang, until we arrive in Honolulu or Bangkok. Is that correct?" Captain Tan was never quite sure what Chang's plans were.

"You are correct, my dear captain. After the bomb

explodes and the confusion begins, the two agents will depart from here in an inconspicuous manner. Jacque and Mr. Kochark must make their own plans. Neither one is connected in any way to the bombing. You will not see me until I arrive back in Asia, or possibly in Honolulu. I do not know when that will be myself."

It was not quite the truth. Chang would not include the small, but not insignificant point that he had ordered Jacque to dispose of the two agents when it became convenient.

He had already arranged for credentials that would link the two agents to a domestic terrorist group. He had a busy schedule planned for himself. He left the *Malaga Badra* and departed.

THURSDAY, SEPTEMBER 10

ON THURSDAY, SAM GREEN LEFT DETROIT AND FLEW TO THE Chippewa County Regional Airport near Sault Ste. Marie. A private plane flew him to Mackinac Island. He rode a Percheron driven carriage to the Mission Point Resort. The management had assigned him a suite of two adjoining rooms that were close to the lobby. It would serve as his control center, and would be only seconds away from the large meeting rooms that the new Conservative Party would use. The Saturday night banquet would be held at the Grand Hotel, but all of the other meetings were being held at Mission Point.

Sam walked over to answer the door of his suite. "Come on in Reino. I called Bradley, too. He should be here shortly."

Brad arrived at Sam's suite a few minutes after Reino. Sam was talking. "I have agents placed in both the Grand and here at Mission Point. We don't know what to expect, yet. We just assume that the Saturday night banquet will be the crucial time. I wish we were certain."

Brad waited for a break in Sam's directions to them before he spoke. "I just got back from Hawaii as you both know, and I met with George, naturally. He told me that he placed an INS member, by the name of Kochark, in the ODAM secret council. He attended his first ODAM meeting back in July, in Bangkok."

Brad continued, "George said that Kochark made a reservation at the Grand Hotel. He'll use the name Edgar Kozar from Bangkok. He thinks.... no.... he is sure.... that they plan on disposing of the Chinese foreign minister.

He wants you to contact him at the Grand Hotel, Sam. He will have the latest information on Chang Hai's plan. But be careful not to expose Kochark's connection with us. George said it would be disastrous if his true identity were discovered by Chang Hai, or by Jacque Kamel. George is certain that Jacque will be in either the Grand or Mission Point."

"Thanks, Brad. I'll make an attempt to contact Kochark tomorrow, without exposing him. Jacque will certainly not use his own name at the hotel, so my team will do a computer search to identify late reservations at both of them. If we locate him, we can watch every move he makes."

22.

◆ A GROUP OF CONGRESSMEN AND WOMEN FROM BOTH parties who were interested in the new Conservative Party were boarding the Shepler's, Star Line, and Arnold Line ferries at the Mackinaw City docks to go to the Island. Nate Goodrich, the junior senator from Grand Rapids, Michigan, was hosting a group of about thirty people, including families.

Governor Dan Broadwell was waiting at the Mackinac Island Chamber of Commerce Building, in the center of town, for the group. Nate spotted the Governor first.

"Hello Dan, you'll notice that I took the boat instead of flying in. Remember two years ago my plane almost didn't make it on the take off?"

"Yes, I recall that it scared the heck out of all of us."

The Governor pointed, "All of you should board the Mission Point carriage. It's over there."

He turned to Nate. "You and Paul Bunche and I will have a short organization meeting at three this afternoon."

Nate asked, "How many total members do we have signed up, Dan?"

"Forty-eight registered. With their families there are about twice that number. I'd say about a hundred. A few are not coming until tomorrow."

The senator stopped to watch a team of four monstrous Belgians pulling one of the longer carriages. He had promised his wife and daughter that he would take them on the Island tour tomorrow. "How about Chong Lo Pan? When is he coming, Dan?"

"Sam Green, the FBI director down state.... you know Sam, don't you?"

"Sure, I know Sam Green. I've had to work with him a few times."

Governor Broadwell continued, "Well, Sam went to the Chippewa County Regional Airport, you remember, the old Kincheloe Air Force Base, to meet Chong Lo Pan and his party. An Air Force jet is bringing them into that airport because it has the long 12,000 -foot runway. The runways here are too short for the big jets. Chong informed me that he has a small party of six people with him."

The Governor stopped to look at his watch. "They should be here shortly. They'll come in from the St. Ignace side. I arranged for a suite for him, and two other rooms for his party at the Grand. I thought it was strange he didn't want a separate room for his secretary. If he were an American.... or a Frenchman.... I wouldn't have thought it strange. Now I'm anxious to see what his secretary looks like."

O

JUST BEFORE MIDNIGHT THE *MALAGA BADRA* HAD REACHED THE Mackinac Bridge. The American Lake Pilot, Rick Slaker, was sleeping in his cabin on the upper deck. He had developed intense stomach pains shortly after he had a cup of coffee in the mess hall. Captain Tan had suggested that he should relax, and have a cup of coffee, just one hour before they were scheduled to arrive at the Straits.

A foreign ship was not required to notify the Coast Guard when it arrived at the Straits of Mackinac. It was a matter of courtesy, however, and Captain Tan knew the protocol of the Great Lakes. It was common practice for ship captains to make their position known to the Coast Guard at thirty minutes before the Bridge. This time Captain did not notify the Coast Guard.

At five minutes before midnight he slowed the engines to a snail's pace, and coasted through the two lighthouses in front of Mackinac Island. The old wooden hulled Chris-Craft pulled up close to the *Malaga Badra* as the Jacob's ladder came sliding down. Jacque was alone at the wheel of the Chris-Craft. The two men climbed down the rope ladder. Their suitcases were then slowly dropped down to the deck of the cabin cruiser, at the end of a rope. The cruiser eased away toward the marina. A few minutes later Captain Tan increased the speed of his engines back to normal.

Jacque was proud of his 1960, thirty-two foot antique wooden Chris-Craft, which he had just displayed at the annual Les Cheneaux Islands Antique Wooden Boat Show near the towns of Hessel and Cedarville in August. He moved slowly into his berth at the Mackinac Island marina. No one paid any attention to the three men as one of Jacque's bodyguards drove them to the Mission Point Resort in a small carriage pulled by two frisky Clydesdales. They didn't have to register or pass through the main lobby. Jacque had taken care of everything so that they could drive right up to the room in one of the former college dormitories.

On Saturday morning Jacque's carriage transported the two men to the Grand Hotel. They were dressed as typical Grand Hotel tourists, which means that they displayed a sophisticated and expensive selection of name brand clothing. They checked into the room, which was selected carefully by Jacque to be on the lower floor.

The man called Anwar spoke to the Irishman, with an obvious tone of disdain, "I have helped you carry the package Mr. Shannon. Don't you want me to help you place it?"

Shannon had already made it quite clear that he must go alone to place the bomb in the area selected by Jacque, near the large dining room at the Grand Hotel, that was to be the site of the Saturday night banquet.

"I must go alone. We cannot take any chances, and I explained that I only work alone. It is my nature."

Anwar despised Shannon, but Chang and Jacque had picked him because of his superior skills. Anwar thought of disposing of him and doing the job himself, but what if he failed? How would he then explain his actions? Shannon picked up the bag with the bomb in it. The bomb was designed to cause a small explosion. Surrounding the explosive was a cartridge with a newly developed chemical weapon that would permeate a large building. It would kill everyone in the immediate confined area within minutes, and quickly throughout the rest of the building, depending on the flow of air.

Jennie had provided Jacque with the general room plan so that he was able to identify the areas that would serve as a hiding place. For the past two days Jacque had been seeking the right location. He had found a storage room that, over the hundred year life of the hotel, had been rebuilt more than once. It had a door in the back that opened into a large closet. The closet was adjacent to and had a large ventilation shaft that opened directly into the dining room.

Shannon waited until no one was in the area, and slipped into the storage room with the bag. Jacque was waiting in the room for him.

"I didn't expect you to be here." Shannon was noticeably disturbed.

"I wanted to be sure that you found the right room. It is not easy to find. I will hand the bomb up to you. Do you want it out of the suitcase."

"No!" Shannon grumbled as he climbed up into the ventilation shaft. Jacque handed the small suitcase with the bomb in it up to him. Shannon crawled close to the wall of the dining room, where he left the bomb.

"I set the timer for eight-thirty, as you wished, Mr. Kamel. Is that right?"

"That is correct, Shannon. The speeches are scheduled to begin at that time."

Jacque had placed some materials around the bomb,

that would be associated with a suspected domestic terrorist group. Jacque and Shannon surreptitiously left the area
and separated.

Jacque had instructed Anwar to kill Shannon. He knew
that after Shannon had placed the bomb, there was no further need for him. What Anwar didn't know was that
Jacque had no intention of actually paying him the $50,000
for the deed. Jacque had promised to give it to him on his
cabin cruiser after the explosion. Jacque's bodyguard would
then dispose of Anwar, and they would drop his body into
Lake Huron.

When Shannon returned to the room Anwar lunged at
him with a knife. Jacque certainly didn't mean for him to do
it in the Grand Hotel, before the explosion, but Anwar's
jealousy had gotten the best of him. He couldn't wait any
longer. Shannon made a quick move that deflected the
knife, so that he received only a minor gash on his left
shoulder. He quickly thrust his right arm around Anwar's
neck and twisted. Snap! His neck broken, Anwar slumped
to the floor.

O

Sam Green asked Reino to contact Kochark, who was
registered as Edgar Kozar. Reino had arranged with the
Assistant Manager, Jake Gibbons, to borrow a waiter's attire.
He waited until Jacque left the room and knocked on the
door.

"Mr. Kozar, you ordered lunch. Here it is."

Kochark let him in, closed the door behind him, and
said, "Identify yourself."

Reino showed him his identification as sheriff, and said, "I know that you are Kochark. Is that enough assurance?"

"Yes." Kochark knew that no one, but one of George's members, would know his true identity.

"What can you tell me Mr. Kochark? We need to act on your directions."

"They have the bomb, all right. It is the latest invention from Saddam's arsenal of chemical devastation. Chang Hai selected a master terrorist from Ireland, named Shannon, to set the bomb. The bomb will go off during the banquet, if we don't stop them. Jacque would never tell me where. Maybe they haven't decided, yet. I can't be too inquisitive or I might arouse suspicion. Come back at least an hour before the banquet begins, and I will tell you more. I must find out where they are going to place it. I'll get it out of Jacque, somehow."

Reino left the room, and disposed of his waiter's uniform. He went to the room that he had registered under the name of Gary Dean. Brad was waiting for him in the room.

O

IT WAS TWO HOURS BEFORE THE BANQUET WAS TO BEGIN. JACQUE went to the room of his two associates. He knocked on the door. No answer. He had a key and opened the door. No one was in the room. He grumbled to himself, and looked around, opening the closet door. The body of Anwar slumped to the floor. Jacque checked his pulse, and was convinced that he was dead. Why did Shannon kill Anwar? He expected the reverse, but not now. Not here at the Grand Hotel!

He had to locate Shannon. Where would he have gone after killing Anwar? He wouldn't stay around with the body in his room. He must have fled. Jacque had made sure that his name was not associated with their rooms. He had always used assumed names. But, that didn't guarantee that someone at the registration desk might not identify him.

He went to Kochark's room. Jacque fully expected that he would have already left the Island, knowing that the bomb would be set to explode during the banquet. He had a key, and entered the room, only to find a pistol pointed at his face. On the other end of the silenced revolver was Kochark.

"It is time to confess, Mr. Kamel. I am not your associate, but your enemy. You will shortly be placed under arrest. We need you to direct us to the bomb. If you do not, you shall die with us."

He picked up the phone and talked to Sam Green. "You may come and arrest Mr. Kamel now."

As he was placing the phone down, Kamel thrust out his leg in a karate move, and knocked the gun out of Kochark's hand. They grappled on the floor in a desperate struggle to grasp the revolver. When the silenced gun went off, Kochark rolled over, blood spurting from his chest. Jacque got up and ran out of the room. His only goal was to get off the Island.

Sam, Reino, and Brad were hurrying toward the room. They saw Jacque leave the room and run down the hall.

Reino said, "I'll get him. You check the room to see what happened to Kochark!"

Reino ran out of the building after Jacque. Jacque ran onto West Bluff Road next to the Grand. He ran past a gazebo, used for weddings, and into the woods. He knew exactly where to cut across to Turkey Hill Road below the Governor's Residence. From there he could slip down to Fort Street and to the marina, where his trusty cabin cruiser was docked.

Sam and Brad entered the hotel room and found Kochark lying on the floor. He moaned quietly; there was blood on his shirt and over the rug. Sam called the operator, "Get me a doctor, quick!"

Historically, motorized vehicles were not allowed on the Island. With so many tourists it became necessary to have motorized vehicles, an ambulance, police car, and fire trucks. The Mackinac Island ambulance was immediately called to the scene. It carried Kochark to the small medical center on Market Street.

O

THE BANQUET HAD BEGUN AT SIX O'CLOCK IN THE LARGE DINING room. Cocktails were served until seven when the dinner was to begin. Governor Dan Broadwell would speak first. Then Paul Bunche, the Governor of Texas would be followed by the Chinese Foreign Minister, Chong Lo Pan.

The group of conservative Republican and Democratic senators, and congressmen and women was present to establish strategy for the November national election. They planned to launch the new Conservative Party, and to pave the way for a successful campaign for the next presidential election. Paul and Dan were determined to stop the spread of terrorism that was being supported and encouraged by anti-American nations and hate groups.

They believed that the American people were fed up with the liberal policies of both parties, and were ready for a new political party based on ethical and moral responsibility. With teenage crime exploding, and gambling becoming the entertainment fetish of the entire nation, a new domestic agenda was critical.

Mainland China and the Asian Pacific Rim countries represented the developing economic markets of the twenty-first century. That was the main theme of their international platform. They also believed that the cooperation of mainland China was needed to stop the transport of surplus military weapons from the former Communist nations to the terrorist groups, and to stop Saddam from developing new chemical weapons.

23.

JACQUE REACHED THE MACKINAC MARINA, WITH Reino still a hundred yards behind. He started the Chris-Craft engine, and sped out of the harbor. Reino reached the dock, spouting off a few words that would probably embarrass his good buddy Bradley!

Back at the Grand Hotel Sam was getting desperate. Kochark was supposed to find out where the bomb was. He was unconscious. Sam had the agents he brought with him searching for the bombers. By tracing the more recent reservations, they had narrowed the possibilities down to two or three rooms.

Then, just moments before Kochark had called him, one of his agents reported that they had found the dead body of a man in a room on the lower level. It now seemed that Jacque was their last resort, and he was trying to escape from Reino. Sam was facing panic. It was now eight o'clock, and he faced making a decision. A decision based on the possibility.... it was still no more than a likely possibility, that a vehicle of man's most despicable and evil contrivance might destroy the lives of some of the nation's most eminent leaders as well as hundreds of innocent people. The weight of that decision was indeed overwhelming. The bomb could go off at any minute. He would have to make the hotel officials attempt to evacuate everyone in the hotel immediately.

"Well, Bradley. This is it. We can't delay any longer. All of our options have been stymied. I must make a decision.... immediately."

Reino returned to tell Sam and Brad that Jacque had escaped. He was out of breath from running up the hill to the Grand.

It was then that an urgent call came in for Professor Bradley Kendall. The desk had trouble locating him.

"Ello, is this the professor, Bradley Kendall?"

"Yes, it is. Who is this speaking?" Brad had an inkling, but would not guess.

"It's yer ol' pal Ian.... 'member in Singapore mate.... it's Ian Gillespie. Or I moight say.... the name is Patrick Shannon!"

"Ian.... why yes.... Ian.... I'm glad to hear from you ....but.... why did you say Patrick Shannon?"

Reino interrupted, shouting, "That's the name of the bomber. Kochark said he's the terrorist who set the bomb!"

The caller continued, "It's me latest moniker, mate! The miserable cusses picked me ta set their firecracker off at 'alf past eight. Whatdaya think a that? It's almost that time now. Any boom there yet, matey?"

"You mean?"

"Sure, mate. Georgy boy an' I fixed 'em bloody well.

We set em up dandy! There's no bomb there, mate. It's not about ta go off. It's roight 'ere with me. I put a dummy bomb in the poke, just so's ol' Jacque would be fooled. Even Kochark didn't know it t'was me. Now tell yer FBI boys to stop worry'in."

"Wait Ian, just a minute, please. Let me be sure I have this right. You mean that you are the so called terrorist named Shannon?"

"Roight, mate. Georgy and I planned it all. He got me the ID with the IRA, and Oi did the rest. It's as simple as that. Tell yer FBI buddy that the real firecracker'll be in Georgy's 'ands, over in 'Onny'lulu by tomorrow. E'll be in charge of it then. Oi only dragged it out this long, so you'd catch them buggars, Jacque and Chang. I 'ope you did, mate."

Brad hated to tell him the truth. "Sorry Ian. Chang never showed up anywhere, and Jacque just got away. But don't worry, Sam and Reino will get him."

Ian told Brad where to find the suitcase with the dummy substitute bomb. He recommended that it be retrieved, so no questions would be asked, in case it was found. That was the end of the substance of the conversation.

"Sam.... Reino.... stop worrying.... there is no bomb."

"Are you sure?" Sam was relieved but skeptical.

"That was Ian Gillespie, the one who saved me in Singapore. He was the IRA terrorist named Patrick Shannon. He and George tricked Chang Hai and Jacque."

"Why did he make us wait so long? Why didn't he tell us in advance so we wouldn't worry?" Sam growled.

"You have to understand George. By nature he's overly

cautious. Getting Ian on the inside must have required absolute secrecy. He desperately wanted to expose both Jacque and Chang Hai. He can't destroy ODAM all at once. It's too widespread in the world. He can chop away at its branches, like nabbing Chang Hai. He probably expected that we would have caught both Jacque and Chang this way."

Brad had been around George much more than either Sam or Reino. He felt that he knew his motives, and some of his strategy.

"Hey, fellas!" Reino recalled. "With all the urgency, I forgot to tell you two that I called the Coast Guard on my cellular phone right after Jacque took off. They are chasing him.... or at least, should be trying to catch him right now."

"What's the plan, Sam?" Brad wondered. "We'd better stop and think about our next move."

Sam pondered a moment. "Let's see. There is no bomb.... are you sure of this Ian Gillespie fellow, Bradley? Our next move depends on his telling the truth."

"He's the one who saved my life when Chang Hai kidnapped me. I know that he's one of George's boys.... or he couldn't have known about Singapore."

"Okay. That means that the danger is over. I'll work with the Coast Guard, and try to get Jacque."

Reino said, "When you catch Jacque, I'll charge him with the murder of the man in the hotel room. He must have done it.... who else?"

"We can't afford to let the news media know about the dead man yet, Reino," Sam said. "Our agreement with the INS, which is approved by the state and federal law enforcement agencies, is to maintain secrecy in cases of a national threat. And when the ODAM terrorists used Saddam's chemical weapons to threaten our congressional leaders and other innocent people, it most certainly qualifies as a national threat."

"All right," Reino said. "I'll handle the details. The body of the man will be taken to our morgue in St. Ignace.

Oscar will examine him, and I'll give you the details of how he died."

"Off hand, Reino one of my men told me that it looks as if his neck was broken.... deliberately, of course," Sam Green added.

"Okay. We'll verify the cause of death, and then take our time with the usual details, until you find out who he is.

He's probably a foreigner, so it'll take plenty of time. My guess is we'll never find out.... officially.... that is."

O

JACQUE HAD MANAGED TO SPEED AWAY FROM REINO AND HEAD eastward around Mackinac Island. He was familiar with the Les Cheneaux Islands, near the towns of Hessel and Cedarville along the lower eastern tip of the Upper Peninsula. Each summer he had displayed his antique wooden Chris-Craft in the competition. He headed straight for Marquette Island, the largest in the chain. He could circle around it, and then find scads of small islands to maneuver around and hide.

Reino had called the Commander of the Coast Guard station in St. Ignace, Perry Grant. Perry had ordered their smallest launch to the area immediately, but Jacque had a sizeable head start. Fortunately, as they left the St. Ignace harbor they spotted him heading toward the Les Cheneaux area.

By the time Jacque circled around Marquette Island the Coast Guard launch was closing the distance between them. While he was looking back, he ran directly into a group of rocks protruding out of the shallow water. Although the Chris-Craft was an antique, the original engine had been replaced with a new more powerful one.

Traveling at full speed, the collision threw him mercilessly into the rocks.

Perry Grant pulled beside the broken craft. Two of his guardsmen jumped into the water to retrieve Jacque's broken body.

"Is he alive?" Perry yelled.

"I don't think so, Sir. It looks like his head was smashed real bad."

They hauled Jacque and themselves on board and headed back to St. Ignace. One of the guardsmen attempted to revive him on the way back, but it was no use.

Jacque was as dead as a door nail.

○

BRAD TOOK THE FERRY TO MACKINAW CITY AND DROVE HIS CAR to the cottage on the Straits. He walked in, and before he turned on the lights he noticed that the red light on the answering machine was blinking once, which meant that there was one message. He pressed the button.

"Professor Kendall. This is your friend. You remember me as your host, the first mate on the *Malaga Badra*. Your lady friend is in no danger. She is a guest of mine at the moment. She will not be harmed before I contact you, which will be very soon. Then I will tell you what you must do to have her returned unharmed." That was the end of the recorded message.

Brad shouted angrily at the answering machine. "Where will you contact me? Here at the cottage? And when? You.... miserable cuss." He looked at the machine as if it should answer him.... but it didn't!

O

BACK IN HAWAII, MADELAINE HAD BEEN AT HER BEACH HOUSE IN Waimanalo. She was leisurely watching the ocean waves splashing on the beautiful sand beach that stretched all the way to Kailua and Kaneohe. The doorbell rang. When she opened the door, the man with a face reminiscent of Peter Lorre said, "Hello Miss Kaleo. Do you remember me? Inspector Jared Mohar, from Kuala Lumpur. I would like to talk with you."

Madelaine panicked when she saw his face. She tried to slam the door shut, but Chang Hai quickly stuck his foot inside to block it from locking. She turned and fled for the door on the ocean side of the beach house. She managed to get outside on the wooden deck, but Chang caught her before she reached the sand. He grabbed her around the neck and held her in a death grasp. Then he injected her with a needle.

24.

AFTER ITS OMINOUS MISSION AT THE STRAITS OF
Mackinac on Friday midnight, the *Malaga Badra*
had continued its voyage to the Soo Locks. It
loaded its cargo of specialty steel at the Algoma Steel
Company at Sault Ste. Marie, Canada. By Saturday night
the ship was on its way down Lake Huron to Detroit. In a
few days it would be through the St. Lawrence Seaway and
into the Atlantic Ocean.

When the *Malaga Badra* was passing through the
Panama Canal, Captain Tan Wo Lin was instructed to call
Chang Hai in Hawaii.

"I heard no mention on the news of the bomb exploding,
Mr. Chang. There would certainly be news of the death of
so many politicians, and the visiting Chinese Foreign
Minister," Captain Tan said.

"You are right, my dear Captain. I am sorry to say that
the bomb did not go off. That Kochark and Jacque Kamel
have failed us. They will pay with their lives for their incom-
petence. I should never have trusted Jacque on such an

important mission. And I never trusted that Kochark when I first met him in Bangkok. Sauloo argued that the ten million dollars that Kochark's backers paid was reason enough for him to observe."

"What happened to the two men sent to place the bomb?" Captain Tan asked.

"I do not understand what could have gone wrong. I selected the Irishman, and the other one myself. And Jacque assured me that his maps and other arrangements were foolproof. I am fearful that Sauloo, and the ODAM leaders may blame me. I must retrieve the unexploded bomb or they will surely have me eliminated. They do not want the technology exposed to the enemy."

◯

WHEN MADELAINE BECAME CONSCIOUS SHE WAS IN A SMALL cabin. She looked out the window and saw the waves. She opened the door and walked out on the deck, feeling dizzy from the drugs that were in her system, and from the motion of the ship. She was on a large yacht. It was a windy day, with six- to eight-foot waves, but she could recognize from the shoreline of Maui that she was on the way to the Big Island of Hawaii.

Chang had kept her drugged until the ship was in the ocean, away from Honolulu Harbor. She climbed the stairway up to the top deck, wondering why no one tried to stop her.

"Good day, Miss Kaleo," the sailor at the wheel, who she presumed to be the ship's captain, greeted her at the open door of the cabin. "I am indeed sorry for the circumstances that brought you here."

Madelaine liked the sailor intuitively. He seemed sincere when he said it.

"Why am I free to move around?"

"Do you wish to jump into the water? I do not think you do. Where else could you escape?"

Chang Hai entered the wheelhouse. "Ah, my dear, Miss Kaleo. You have awakened, as beautiful as ever. How do you feel? I hope you have had no ill effects from my sleeping medicine."

"You are a beast. Why are you kidnapping me?"

"You have good reason to dislike me, but your life also depends on me. You must act like a lady on our cruise in order to stay alive. If you do, you will be allowed to walk freely around the ship."

"Where are you taking me.... and why?"

"You and I will end our voyage at Kona. There you will be set free, unharmed.... if.... and I say again, if .... your friend, Professor Kendall, complies with my request."

Madelaine was bright enough to keep her mouth shut after his explanation. It would do no good to argue with a monster like Chang Hai. And she wasn't quite sure that she wanted to know what Bradley was required to do for her release.

MONDAY, SEPTEMBER 21

ON MONDAY BRAD HAD GONE TO LUNCH WITH REINO. WHEN he and Reino returned to the cottage the message blinker was on.

"My dear Professor. Your sweet Polynesian lady friend is with me in Hawaii. If you want to see her alive you must go to her house in Waimanalo. Be there in three days, that is on Thursday. I will call you at twelve o'clock noon. Be there, alone, to answer the phone. I will tell you where we will meet. You have possession of the weapon that did not explode. You must return it to me unaltered, or your beautiful lady friend will not be returned to you."

"Ye gads. He's a buggar!" Reino exclaimed.

"Ian Gillespie said he has the bomb, with the chemical weapon.... and he told me that he is taking it to George in Hawaii. I wonder if Chang knew that somehow?" Brad questioned rhetorically.

"Does anyone know what the bomb contains, Brad?" Reino asked.

"Not that I know of. It could be a poison gas, or germ warfare. I think that is why Ian took the bomb to George.

He has the resources to have it thoroughly analyzed. The United Nations can use this evidence to deal with Saddam when he denies them access to his palaces."

○

BRAD WAS ON THE UNITED AIRLINES FLIGHT TO HONOLULU ON Wednesday, September twenty-third. He followed his usual pattern of renting a Buick LeSabre from the Alamo Rental Car Agency near the airport. He drove downtown to meet George at the INS office in the old Wo Fat's Chinese Restaurant building. It was made famous by the episodes of "Hawaii Five-O," but was no longer used as a restaurant. The INS had bought it to use as their headquarters.

They didn't change the outside appearance of the nostalgic landmark restaurant.

Ian Gillespie greeted Brad at the door and took him to George's office. "Greetin's mate. Did ya 'ave a good trip 'ere?"

"The flight was a little rough. Probably due to El Nino.

We're blaming everything weather wise on the little boy, aren't we? If they called it La Nina, we could have blamed it on a girl!" Brad exercised some of his humor.

"Oi never thought a that, mate."

George greeted Brad. "Good to see you Bradley. Ian here has given me his version of what happened. Now I would like yours. First, however, would you like a cup of coffee with some hot malasadas?"

"Malasadas.... from the Kapahulu Bakery?"

"Where else. I don't serve them in the Kahana. That's an idea, though. I probably should."

Brad chomped down a couple of warm malasadas before he could talk. He still craved his coffee in spite of the semi-tropical climate in Hawaii.

"Well, George. I don't know where to begin."

"Start with Madelaine. What happened to her?"

"Madelaine wanted to see Michigan, especially the Mackinac tourist area. It was a chance for her to have a vacation. It was hard for me to object.... but I did. I never would have dreamed that she would have been in any danger here in Hawaii. Who would have thought that Chang would have kidnapped her while his big strike was going on at Mackinac Island?"

"Chang Hai knows everything, Bradley. You should

know him by now, after he kidnapped you on the *Malaga Badra.*"

"It had to be a move of desperation only planned after he was certain that the bomb had failed to go off."

"What makes ya think that, matey?"

"Well, Ian. If the bomb had gone off.... and thanks to you and George's smart planning.... it didn't, Chang would have had no reason to kidnap Madelaine. She became his only weapon to force us to give up the bomb."

"I agree, Bradley. He wouldn't have needed her otherwise. Unless.... "

"Unless what, Georgy boy?" The Scottish mind was wondering.

George went on. "The head of ODAM, the man named Sauloo, is plagued by us. He only knows that our organization is based in Hawaii. We have intercepted communications that indicate that ODAM would pay any amount to eliminate their unknown Hawaii adversaries. That's what Chang called the INS, their miserable adversaries. So that means that Chang saw an opportunity, not only to get the bomb back, but to bring us out in the open."

"What can he do to lure you out?"

"He could hold you as a hostage along with Madelaine. He probably assumes that Madelaine doesn't know much about the INS, but that you do. That is why you were kidnapped before."

"Do Sam and Reino know why the bomb didn't go off, Bradley?"

"Yes. When Ian called they were right there in the room. If Ian hadn't called, Sam would have had to evacuate the entire Grand Hotel in minutes. All of a sudden our sources of information disappeared. We expected Kochark to find out where the bomb was to be set. He was unconscious, shot by Jacque. Then we expected to catch Jacque, thinking that he would know. And he escaped."

"That reminds me, Bradley. Earlier today Sam called.

He informed me that Jacque is dead. He was killed trying to escape. Sam said that he will officially report that Jacque killed the ODAM agent, called Anwar. His neck was broken. Sam said it had to be Jacque. He concluded that Jacque was planning to kill both of the bombers, so they would never be able to talk. He killed one of them, Anwar, but the other one got away."

"Oi 'ave a little confession ta make, maties," Ian interjected with a twitch of guilt in his Cockney eye.

George and Brad both looked curiously toward Ian Gillespie.

"Oi'm the bloke who snapped 'is neck, maties. 'E tried ta kill me when oi come back from pretendin' ta set the big firecracker. I 'ad ta snap 'is neck, or oi would'n be 'ere taday."

"That explains it," Brad practically shouted. "Sam couldn't find a plausible reason for Jacque to have killed him, but.... who else? He wanted to hold Jacque for some crime, and that was a logical and convenient one. Sam had no idea who the killer was, except some mysterious terrorist who had disappeared."

George laughed. "So Ian turned out to be the mysterious ODAM terrorist! You fooled them all, Ian."

"It was your plan, Georgy boy. Me job was jus' ta carry it out."

"I am sorry that we couldn't tell you and Sam in advance, Bradley. It had to be completely secretive to assure that ODAM would accept Ian as an IRA terrorist. And it had to be done quickly. We had little time to complete all the credentials, and give him a believable record of accomplishments. Fortunately Ian had the experience, and gained superior skills while he served in the British secret service."

"I understand, George. Anyway, it worked out much better this way. Even though Sam and Reino had to sweat it out for a few hours. They were really stumped near the end. What's funny.... that's not the best word for it.... what's ironic is that the people at the banquet and in the hotel will never know the truth. Except for Governor Broadwell, the others will never know how close they were to meeting their maker. They would surely want to thank you and Ian if they knew."

"That is what the INS stands for, Bradley. Stopping international terrorists. They are spreading too fast. This technology, like Saddam's chemical weapons and the availability of more powerful portable bombs, is threatening a peaceful world. If we don't get tougher with the drug dealers, we'll never succeed. Singapore says death to drug traffickers and they mean it. Then some Americans actually criticized Singapore for spanking one of their teenagers with a stick. While he was in the Singapore jail more than one thousand American teenagers died from drunk drivers and drugs. That kind of reasoning by the mainlanders is what makes it difficult to stop crime."

"I know," Brad said. "When the mainland Americans

stopped the good, sensible parents from spanking their kids, teenage crime multiplied. Now the undisciplined children have become criminals. Teenagers at eleven years old have become killers. When children were disciplined, sensibly, they understood how important authority is. Now the police are called *cops*. And older people are called *guys*."

Brad was getting all wound up. "When I was a child, my mother said that if you dressed like a bum, you would act like a bum. And boy was she right. Now the teenagers dress like clowns, and they act accordingly. Television has destroyed all respect for authority. They blame everything on the government."

"Don't major network announcers, like Tom, Peter, or Dan, know that the people *are* the government? Our single vote is the only source of a free government. We, the people, are the government. How can any American forget it? Whenever television announcers blame the government for something, they should point to themselves. Then they would be telling the truth. By a single vote we authorized Bill Clinton to be President. Even if we didn't vote for him, we agreed to abide by a majority. That is America. And all the world knows that our system works. Along with the other free republics, like Canada, it is the most successful system of government in modern history."

Ian and George clapped jokingly at the spontaneous tirade of the articulate, but very conservative, professor. At least he wasn't the absent-minded professor.

George changed the subject. "Did Chang tell you what you are to do, Bradley?"

Brad descended from his high horse. "This is what

Chang said, 'Go to Madelaine's house in Waimanalo and wait for him to call at noon tomorrow.' "

"Then do exactly what Chang asks. If he wants you to meet him somewhere, he will probably demand that you go alone. So you know you can depend on Ian. If it's possible he will be somewhere close by."

George didn't tell Brad that he and Ian already knew where Chang's plane had landed. The INS computers had traced it for them. The call to Brad would verify their information. George always tried to stay one step ahead of his adversaries.

25.

◆ BRAD HAD DRIVEN FROM WO FAT'S, IN DOWNTOWN Honolulu, over to the Pali Highway. He had heard in the news that the new highway H3, which provided access from the Leeward side to the Windward side of Oahu, was open in late 1997. It apparently was started thirty-eight years ago.

During the construction period it had many problems. On the Windward side it had infringed upon sacred Hawaiian burial grounds.

Even the military reason for its need was changed. He remembered that it ended at the entrance to the Kaneohe Marine Base, where he had taught graduate classes for Central Michigan University. It was originally touted as a route for military vehicles during the cold war period.

In 1960, the USSR leader, Nikita Kruschev, warned the United States, "We will bury you!" People sometimes forget those facts of history. The worry about the Communist threat was much greater back then, thought Brad.

He drove along Kaneohe Bay Drive to Kailua and on Kalanianaole Highway to Waimanalo. Madelaine had given him a key on his last visit. He had a restless night. The morning went slowly, while he waited for Chang to call at noon. The call was right on time.

"Professor Kendall. Your lady friend and I are on the Big Island near Kona. You are to carry the suitcase with you to the Kona Airport. I have made a reservation for you on the Aloha Airlines flight that leaves the Honolulu Airport at three-fifteen today. When you arrive, remain at the Aloha Airlines desk until a man asks for you. When he shows you a passport with my name on it, you must follow him with the suitcase. The missile must not have been altered, or your lady friend will not be released to you alive." He hung up before Brad could ask any questions.

○

BRAD IMMEDIATELY REPORTED THE CALL FROM CHANG TO George. He then carried the suitcase into the car and hurried to the airport. His flight on Aloha Airlines to Kona left on time.

He waited at the Aloha desk for fifteen minutes before Chang's bodyguard approached him. Brad would not hand him the suitcase until he produced Madelaine. They walked out to Chang's private jet. When Chang Hai appeared at the bottom of the stairs, the bodyguard pulled out a gun and stuck it in Brad's back.

Chang said, "Professor, come over here. When my associate has examined the contents of the suitcase to his satisfaction he will let me know. In the meantime get inside the plane."

"You promised that if I produced the suitcase with the bomb intact, that you would release Madelaine. You must keep your word, Chang. Your gods will not be kind to you, if you do not."

"You are right, my dear professor, there is no need to kill such a beautiful lady. I have no further use for her." He signaled the pilot at the top of the stairs, who then roughly dragged Madelaine out of the plane.

"As soon as we take off, my dear, you may do as you please," Chang said .

Madelaine shouted, with tears smearing what little makeup she had left on her face, "Let him go. You have no reason to hold him. He is just an accounting professor.

He has nothing to do with any of this.... business.... or, whatever it is you're in. Let him go.... Please!"

"I am sorry, my dear. He will tell us who our Hawaiian adversaries are. He is far more knowledgeable than you think, or are willing to admit," Chang spewed.

At that moment a motorized cart filled with suitcases pulled up alongside Chang's airplane. A porter jumped off and said to Chang, "Ai'r these yer suitcases, Sir?"

"No. You have the wrong plane." Chang grumbled at the man.

Brad sensed a brogue of some sort, but couldn't quite place it. All of a sudden, the porter struck the bodyguard's arm, knocking the gun to the ground. He smashed his fist into Chang's face. Chang fell back over the stairs. The porter picked up the gun, grabbed Madelaine by the arm, and ran toward the airport, yelling to Brad, "Come on matey. Run fer yer life!"

Chang and his men rushed onto the plane, and taxied down the runway. They had already been cleared for take-off in a matter of minutes. Five minutes later the plane sailed away into the air and out of sight.

"Ian. You didn't fool me for a minute.... well.... maybe a minute or two, but that's all. That fake beard and clumsy looking hat had me fooled. You did it again. Always saving my life."

Madelaine hugged Brad and squeezed him tight. "Oh, I was so worried. He's a monster. He would have killed you for sure. I heard him talking on the yacht with the Captain. He said they would torture you until you told them who the leader of the Hawaii group is. And then they would, in Chang's words, dispose of you."

She switched over to Ian. "Oh you nice man, you. You saved us both."

Ian smiled in ecstasy as Madelaine hugged and squeezed him, too. Brad stood there with a grin on his face, knowing full well how good old Ian must have been enjoying himself. What a reward!

O

THE NEXT DAY ON FRIDAY, SAM GREEN AND REINO ASUMA FLEW into Honolulu and checked in at the Polynesian Hotel. On Saturday night Sam, Reino, Brad, and Ian Gillespie were sitting at the House Without A Key munching on appetizers. It was seven-thirty. They were watching a beautiful

Hawaiian girl dancing the slow, expressive hula to the music of *Sweet Leilani.*

"George should be here to celebrate," Reino said.

Sam said, "You know that George can't be seen with us. He has to remain low key in order to survive."

"Oi kinda watch over Georgy boy when Oi'm in town mates. But, Oi'm not always 'ere."

Sam said, "Tell Reino and me what happened over on the Big Island, Brad. When Reino and I had our meeting with George, he told us you had a close call."

"It would have been if it weren't for Ian here," Brad replied.

It was intermission time. The beautiful Polynesian dancer walked directly over to their table. The men stood up for the lady. She gave Brad a hug. Reino held out his arms for a hug, too. She ended up giving them all a squeeze.

Sam said, "I could watch you dance all night Madelaine.... I mean Hokulani."

Reino blurted, "You mean all week, Sam. This is heaven. You and I would make a good team, Madelaine. Don't waste your time on Bradley. Professors are in the clouds all the time. And accounting professors are the worst when it comes to finance. Brad here would be adding up the cost of your muu'muu's. He would probably make you wear little skimpy ones just to save money."

They all laughed at Reino's facetious proposal.

Brad countered, "Don't listen to him, Madelaine. If you married Reino, he would drive you all over the Upper Peninsula, remember? Manistique to Escanaba, then to Marquette, and way up to Copper Harbor. And then back around to the Straits. Five hundred miles. He'd drive you crazy."

Madelaine laughed, "The eight miles around Mackinac Island in a horse driven carriage would be enough for me."

"Who said anything about marriage, Brad? She'd just be my girlfriend," Reino said almost seriously.

"How come you're dancing tonight, Madelaine? It's a little soon after your terrible ordeal with that miserable Chang, isn't it?" Brad asked.

"This is the best relaxation for me. I enjoy dancing so much. If you ever have too much stress, just dance the hula. It will relax you."

Reino stood up and tried to imitate Madelaine's dance movements. "I just can't wiggle like you, Madelaine."

They all agreed with Reino about that. "You're about as smooth as a bull moose," Brad joked.

Sam reminded them, "You were going to tell Reino and me about your climax on the Big Island with Chang Hai, but first I'll tell you what happened in Mackinac after you left."

"George probably told you that Perry Grant of the Coast Guard chased Jacque. He crashed over in the Les Cheneaux Islands and was killed. That takes care of the murder of the other terrorist. I can close the case by reporting that Jacque killed him."

Brad and Ian didn't say a word about who really killed the terrorist. It was better this way.

"How about the ODAM leader in Chicago, Sam?" Brad asked. "Was there anything further on who it was? You know what I mean.... was it that Hilda woman?"

"Nothing surfaced. It appears to be all just a rumor.

ODAM is smuggling drugs and automatic weapons into Chicago, but that operation appears to be unrelated to the bomb attempt. That's my opinion right now," Sam said.

"By the way. Kochark is recovering nicely. He will be leaving the hospital on Monday and plans to fly to Honolulu for a rest. He works for George, too, you know."

Madelaine said, "It's a shame that Chang got away. He was such a monster. I won't tell all the nasty things he said to me. He tried to get me to.... you know.... the usual thing that men want from me."

"No! I don't know," Reino blurted out. "Tell me what men want from you Madelaine. Tell me all about it."

"Oh! You nasty beast." She kicked Reino in the leg as she laughed.

"Did he try to.... force himself on you, Madelaine?" Brad asked, bringing seriousness back to the conversation.

"No. I was surprised that he didn't. He had the opportunity on the ship. But the nice Captain seemed to be around whenever Chang pressed me. It was as if he were trying to protect me."

"Well, we're lucky for that," Brad concluded.

"Is there any way you can nail Chang Hai, Sam?"

"I don't think so. He's out of our jurisdiction, now. And it would be impossible to pin a crime on him with our liberal system."

"And there'd be plenty of loopholes that some fancy lawyer could find," Reino opined.

Ian Gillespie, who had been just sitting back and enjoying the conversation and the company, especially the female part, finally piped up.

"Oi wasn't goin' to say anythin' mates, but Oi guess now that Oi'd better. When Chang's airyplane was on the ground at Kona, I was the one who filled 'er up with gas. Oi 'ad to pay a pretty penny to bribe the regular feller. Oi'm pretty good with them firecrackers ya realize, so's Oi planted one in the tail section of Chang's airyplane."

Reino butted in, giving Ian a chance to munch on his appetizers and drink some more tea. "By a firecracker, I assume you mean some kind of a small conventional bomb?"

"Roight laddie. I set the cracker to go off when the airyplane was over the deepest part of the Pacific. Ya know.... on the way to Singapore and Bangkok. That's where them boys was 'eadin'. The tail section will fall off, an' the 'ole bunch of 'em will end up fourteen thousan' feet under the drink. Saddam's new chemical firecracker an' all. So it'll never be used by dear ol' Saddam.... or by any of 'is chums."

Sam was flabbergasted. "You mean....? That would have been yesterday. Do you mean that Chang and the bomb are already disposed of?"

"And there's no more worry about the bomb?" Reino added.

"Roight, maties. Changy boy an' 'is chums won't bother us any more. Georgy was convinced that Chang would never stop until 'e killed the perfesser 'ere and 'is lassie. They were 'is only clue to uncover the INS. You fellers, an' Georgy, an' I are the only ones who will ever know the truth. An' we won't tell anyone. Will we maties?"

The group agreed with Ian, and celebrated the rest of the

ABOUT THE AUTHOR

Ronald J. Lewis resides in Mackinaw City, Michigan with his wife, Margaret. They have three children, Jeffrey, Randall, and Gary.

In 1965, Lewis received a Ph.D. in accounting and finance from Michigan State University, and he became the first Acting Dean of the new School of Business at Northern Michigan University. In 1969, he became Dean of Business at Tri-State University in Indiana, and was appointed Vice-President of Academic Affairs at Tri-State in 1973.

During his academic career he wrote two accounting textbooks, and two post-graduate accounting books for his lectures in Singapore and Malaysia. He spent his last ten academic years at Central Michigan University.

Mr. Lewis was listed in *Outstanding Educators in America* in 1972, and in *Who's Who in the Midwest* in 1977, 1989, and 1991.

Not until his retirement in 1992, did Mr. Lewis begin writing mystery novels as a way to relax from the analytical rigor of accounting.

evening watching Madelaine dance in the last show. After they parted and said their farewells, Brad drove Madelaine home to Waimanalo.

"Come in for a few minutes, Bradley."

"Okay, but not for long. You must be exhausted."

She looked straight into his eyes. Her arms went out to him and they melted together. They held each other tight for a long time, it seemed. They kissed softly, with passion.

"Madelaine, you know how much I like you. I want you to be my...."

"You mean you want me to be something like a..... shall we say.... a girlfriend?" Madelaine was trying to be funny, but Brad was dead serious.

"Right. When I come to Hawaii.... which will be more often from now on.... I want to go out with you.... only you. And I don't have any.... you know.... like a girlfriend.... back in Michigan. I'm a professor you know. I'm too busy to have girlfriends," he said that with a mischievous smile, finally realizing that Madelaine was teasing him.

"And you are my only boyfriend, Bradley. I will come to visit you in Mackinaw City. We will go to Mackinac Island.... and we will ride in the carriage, drawn by those wonderful horses. And we will..... !"

She stopped and gave him a vivacious smile. "We are just dreaming.... aren't we Professor Kendall?"

"Maybe Madelaine. But it's fun. And I know that we'll get together.... some day."

"I do too, Bradley my dear. But.... we'll think about that..... tomorrow!"

ADDITIONAL INFORMATION

If you are unable to obtain a copy of *Terror at the Soo Locks*, *Murder in Mackinac*, or *Mackinaw-Honolulu Connection*, or if you would like to contact the author or publisher, please use the following address:

Ronald J. Lewis
c/o Agawa Press
P.O. Box 39
Mackinaw City, Michigan 49701
(616) 436-7032